RAINY DAY KISSES

BY

DEBBIE MACOMBER

MILLS & BOON®

First published in Great Britain 1997
Harlequin Mills & Boon Limited,
Eton House, 18-24 Paradise Road, Richmond, Surrey, TW9 1SR

© Debbie Macomber 1990

ISBN 0 263 80468 2

Set in Times Roman 10 on 12 pt.
02-9711-50331 C

Printed and bound in Great Britain
by Mackays of Chatham PLC, Chatham

Susannah picked up the phone. "This is Susannah Simmons."

"Good morning, beautiful. I just woke up and was lying here thinking how nice it would be if we could escape for the day. Could I tempt you with a drive to the ocean? We could dig for clams, build a sandcastle, and then make a fire and sing our favorite camp songs."

"Listen, Nate, I really am busy. I do have to work late. The fact is, I can't go outside and play today."

"Ouch," Nate cried. "That hurt."

"Perhaps it hit too close to home."

A short silence followed. As crazy as it seemed, spending the afternoon with Nate at the beach sounded far too appealing. The way he made her think and feel was almost frightening. The man was putting her entire career in jeopardy.

Something had to be done, only Susannah wasn't sure what.

Debbie Macomber is one of the most popular romance authors writing today. She's written more than seventy romances and several best-selling 'mainstream' women's fiction novels. Not surprisingly, Debbie has won a number of awards for her books. She lives in Washington State with her husband, Wayne, and their dog, Peterkins. They have four grown children—and a granddaughter, Jazmine Lynne.

Debbie loves to hear from readers. You can reach her at PO Box 1458, Port Orchard, Washington 98366, USA.

Recent titles by the same author:

FALLING FOR HIM
ENDING IN MARRIAGE
THE BACHELOR PRINCE
THE WAY TO A MAN'S HEART

CHAPTER ONE

SUSANNAH SIMMONS BLAMED her sister, Emily, for this. As far as she was concerned this weekend was going to be the nightmare on Western Avenue. Emily, a nineties version of the "earth mother," had asked Susannah, the dedicated career woman, to baby-sit nine-month-old Michelle.

"Emily, I don't know." Susannah had balked when her sister first phoned. What did she, a twenty-eight-year-old business executive, know about babies? The answer was simple—not much.

"I'm desperate."

Her sister must have been to ask her. Everyone knew what Susannah was like around babies—not just Michelle, but infants in general. Unfortunately Susannah just wasn't the motherly type. Interest rates, negotiations, troubleshooting, staff motivation, these were her strong points. Not formula, teething and diapers.

It was nothing short of astonishing that the same two parents could have produced such completely different daughters. Susannah figured that cases such as theirs would baffle even the genetic experts. Emily baked her own oat-bran muffins, subscribed to *Organic Gardening* and hung her wash to dry on a clothesline—even in winter.

Susannah, on the other hand, wasn't the least bit domestic and had no intention of ever cultivating the trait.

She was too busy with her career to let such tedious tasks disrupt her corporate life-style. She was currently serving as a junior vice president in charge of marketing for H&J Lima, the nation's largest sporting goods company. The position occupied almost every minute of her time.

Susannah Simmons was a woman on the rise. Her name kept cropping up in trade journals as an up-and-coming achiever. None of that mattered to Emily, however, who needed a baby-sitter.

"You know I wouldn't ask you if it wasn't an emergency," Emily had pleaded.

Susannah could feel herself weakening. Emily was, after all, her younger sister. "Surely, there's got to be someone better qualified."

Emily hesitated, then tearfully blurted, "I don't know what I'll do if you won't take Michelle." She began to sob pitifully. "Robert's left me."

"What?" If Emily hadn't gained her full attention earlier, she did now. If her sister was an earth mother, then her brother-in-law, Robert Davidson, was Abraham Lincoln, as solid and upright as a thirty-foot oak. "I don't believe it."

"It's true," Emily wailed. "He...he claims I give Michelle all my attention and that I never have enough energy left to be a decent wife." She paused long enough to suck in a quavery breath. "I know he's right...but being a good mother demands so much time and effort."

"I thought Robert wanted six children."

"He does...or did." Emily's sobbing began anew.

"Oh, Emily, it can't be that bad," Susannah murmured in a soothing voice, thinking as fast as she could. "I'm sure you misunderstood Robert. He loves you and

Michelle, and I'm sure he has no intention of leaving you."

"He does," Emily went on to explain between hiccuping sobs. "He asked me to find someone to watch Michelle for a while. He says we have to have some time to ourselves, or our marriage is dead."

That sounded drastic enough to Susannah.

"I swear to you, Susannah, I've called everyone who's ever baby-sat Michelle before, but no one is available. No one—not even for one night. When I told Robert I hadn't found a sitter, he got so angry... and you know that's not like Robert."

Susannah did know. The man was the salt of the earth. Not once in the five years she'd known him could she recall him even raising his voice.

"He said if I didn't take this weekend trip to San Francisco with him he was going alone. I tried to find someone to watch Michelle," Emily went on. "I honestly tried, but there's no one else, and now Robert's home and he's loading up the car and, Susannah, he's serious. He's going to leave without me and from the amount of luggage he's taking, I don't think he intends to come back."

The tale of woe barely skimmed the surface of Susannah's mind. The key word that stayed and planted itself in fertile ground was the word *weekend*. "I thought you said you only needed me for one night?" she gasped.

It was then that Susannah should have realized she wasn't much brighter than a brainless mouse, innocently nibbling away at the cheese in a steel trap.

Emily sniffled once more, probably for effect, Susannah thought darkly.

"We'll be flying back to Seattle early Sunday afternoon. Robert's got some business in San Francisco Saturday morning, but the rest of the weekend is free...and it's been such a long time since we've been alone."

"Two days and two nights," Susannah said slowly, mentally tabulating the hours.

"Oh, please, Susannah, my whole marriage is at stake. You've always been such a good big sister. I know I don't deserve anyone as good as you."

Silently Susannah agreed.

"Somehow I'll find a way to repay you," Emily continued.

Susannah pushed the hair from her face and closed her eyes. Her sister's idea of repaying her was usually freshly baked zucchini bread shortly after Susannah announced she was watching her weight.

"Susannah, please!"

It was then that Susannah had caved in to the pressure. "All right. Go ahead and bring Michelle over."

Somewhere in the distance, she could have sworn she heard the echo of a mousetrap slamming shut.

By the time Emily and Robert had deposited their offspring at Susannah's condominium, her head was swimming with instructions. After planting a juicy kiss on her daughter's rosy cheek, Emily handed the clinging Michelle to a reluctant Susannah.

That was when the nightmare began in earnest.

As soon as her sister left, Susannah could feel herself tense up. Even as a teenager, she hadn't done a lot of baby-sitting; it wasn't that she didn't like children, but kids just didn't seem to take to her.

Holding the squalling infant on her hip, Susannah paced while her mind buzzed with everything she was supposed to remember. She knew what to do in case of diaper rash, colic and several other minor emergencies, but Emily hadn't said one word about to keep Michelle from crying.

"Shhh," Susannah cooed, gently jiggling her niece against her hip. She swore the child had a cry Tarzan would envy.

After the first five minutes, her calm cool composure was cracking under the pressure. She could be in real trouble here. The tenant agreement she'd signed specifically stated "no children."

"Hello, Michelle, remember me?" Susannah asked, doing everything she could think of to quiet the youngster. Dear Lord, didn't the kid need to breathe? "I'm your Auntie Susannah, the business executive."

Her niece wasn't impressed. Pausing only long enough to gulp for air, Michelle increased her volume and glared at the door as if she expected her mother to miraculously appear if she cried long and hard enough.

"Trust me, kid, if I knew a magic trick that'd make your mother reappear, I'd use it now."

Ten minutes. Emily had been gone a total of ten minutes. Susannah was seriously considering giving the state Children's Protective Services a call and claiming that a stranger had abandoned a baby on her doorstep.

"Mommy will be back soon," Susannah murmured wistfully.

Michelle screamed louder. Susannah started to worry about her stemware. The kid's voice was pitched high enough to shatter glass.

More torturous minutes passed, each one an eternity. Susannah was desperate enough to sing. Not knowing any appropriate lullabies, she started off with a couple of ditties from her childhood, but quickly exhausted those. Michelle didn't seem to appreciate them anyway. Since Susannah didn't keep up with the current top twenty, the best she could do was an old Christmas favorite. Somehow singing "Jingle Bells" in the middle of September didn't feel right.

"Michelle," Susannah pleaded, willing to stand on her head if it would keep the baby from wailing, "your mommy will be back, I assure you."

Michelle apparently didn't believe her.

"How about if I buy municipal bonds and put them in your name?" Susannah tried next. "Tax-free bonds, Michelle! This is an offer you shouldn't refuse. All you need to do is stop crying. Oh, please stop crying."

Evidently Michelle wasn't interested.

"All right," Susannah cried, growing desperate. "I'll sign over my IBM stock. That's my final offer, so you'd better grab it while I'm in a generous mood."

Michelle answered by gripping Susannah's collar with both of her chubby fists and burying her wet face in a once spotless white silk blouse.

"You're a tough nut to crack, Michelle Margaret Davidson," Susannah muttered, gently patting her niece's back as she paced. "You want blood, don't you, kid? You aren't going to be satisfied with anything less."

A half hour after Emily had left, Susannah was ready to resort to tears herself. She'd started singing again, some of the ageless Christmas songs. "You'd better watch out,/ you'd better not cry,/ Aunt Susannah's here telling you why...."

She was just starting to really get into the lyrics when someone knocked heavily on her door.

Like a thief caught in the act, Susannah hunched her shoulders and whirled around, fully expecting the caller to be the building superintendent. No doubt there had been complaints and he'd come to confront her.

Expelling a weary sigh, Susannah realized she was defenseless. The only option left to her was to throw herself on his mercy. She squared her shoulders and walked across the lush carpet, prepared to do exactly that.

Only it wasn't necessary. The building superintendent wasn't the person standing on the other side of her door. It was her new neighbor, wearing a baseball cap and a faded T-shirt, and looking more than a little disgruntled.

"The crying and the baby I can take," he said, crossing his arms and relaxing against the doorframe, "but your singing has got to go."

"Very funny," she grumbled.

"The kid's obviously distressed about something."

Susannah glared at him. "Nothing gets past you, does it?"

"Do something."

"I'm trying." Apparently Michelle didn't appreciate this stranger any more than Susannah did because she buried her face in Susannah's collar and rubbed it vigorously back and forth. That at least helped muffle her cries, but there was no telling what it would do to white silk. "I offered her my IBM stock and it didn't do any good," Susannah explained. "I was even willing to throw in my municipal bonds."

"You offered her stocks and bonds, but did you suggest dinner?"

"Dinner?" Susannah echoed. She hadn't thought of that. Emily claimed she'd fed Michelle, but Susannah vaguely remembered something about a bottle.

"The poor thing's probably starving."

"I think she's supposed to have a bottle," Susannah said. She turned and glanced at the assorted bags Emily and Robert had deposited in her condominium along with the necessary baby furniture. From the number of items stacked on the floor, it looked as if she'd been granted permanent guardianship. "There must be one in all this paraphernalia."

"I'll look—you keep the kid quiet."

Susannah nearly laughed out loud. If she was able to keep Michelle quiet, he wouldn't be here in the first place. She imagined she could convince CIA agents to hand over top-secret documents more easily than she could silence one distressed nine-month-old infant.

Without waiting for an invitation, her neighbor moved into the living room. He picked up one of the three overnight bags and rooted through that. He hesitated when he pulled out a stack of freshly laundered diapers, and glanced at Susannah. "I didn't know anyone used cloth diapers anymore."

"My sister doesn't believe in anything disposable."

"Smart woman."

Susannah made no comment, and within a few seconds noted that he'd found a plastic bottle. He removed the protective cap and handed the bottle to Susannah, who looked at it and blinked. "Shouldn't the milk be heated?"

"It's room temperature, and frankly, at this point I don't think the kid's going to care."

He was right. The instant Susannah placed the rubber nipple in her niece's mouth, Michelle gripped the bottle with both hands and sucked at it greedily.

For the first time since her mother had left, Michelle stopped crying. The silence was pure bliss. Susannah's tension eased, and she released a sigh that went all the way through her body.

"You might want to sit down," he suggested next.

Susannah did, and with Michelle cradled awkwardly in her arms, leaned against the back of the sofa, trying not to jostle her charge.

"That's better, isn't it?" Her neighbor tipped the baseball cap farther back on his head, looking pleased with himself.

"Much better." Susannah smiled shyly up at him, studying him for the first time. As far as looks went, her new neighbor was downright handsome. She supposed most women would find his mischievous blue eyes and dark good looks appealing. He was tanned, but she'd have wagered a month's pay that his bronzed features weren't the result of any machine. He obviously spent a good deal of time out-of-doors, which led her to the conclusion that he didn't work. At least not in an office. And frankly, she doubted he was employed outside of one, either. The clothes he wore and the sporadic hours he kept had led her to speculate earlier about her neighbor. If he had money, which he apparently did or else he wouldn't be living in this condominium complex, then he'd inherited it.

"I think it's time I introduced myself," he said conversationally, sitting on the ottoman across from her. "I'm Nate Townsend."

"Susannah Simmons," she said, holding out her hand for him to shake. "I apologize for all the racket. My niece and I are just getting acquainted and—oh boy—it's going to be a long weekend, so bear with us."

"You're baby-sitting for the weekend?"

"Two days and two nights." It sounded like a whole lifetime to Susannah. "My sister and her husband are off on a second honeymoon. Normally my parents would watch Michelle and love doing it, but they're visiting friends in Florida.''

"It was kind of you to offer."

Susannah thought it best to correct the impression. "Trust me, I didn't volunteer for this. In case you hadn't noticed, I'm not very motherly."

"You've got to support her back a little better," he said, watching Michelle.

Susannah tried to do as he suggested, but it felt awkward to hold on to her niece, the bottle and everything else.

"You're doing fine."

"Sure," Susannah muttered. She felt like someone with two left feet who'd been unexpectedly ushered onto center stage and told to perform the lead in *Swan Lake*.

"Relax, will you?" Nate encouraged.

"I told you already I'm not into this motherhood business," she snapped. "If you think you can do any better, you feed her."

"You're doing great. Don't worry about it."

She wasn't doing great at all, and she knew it, but this was as good as she got.

"When was the last time you had anything to eat?" he asked.

"I beg your pardon?"

"You sound hungry to me."

"Well, I'm not," Susannah said irritably.

"I think you are, but don't worry, I'll take care of that." He walked boldly into her kitchen and paused in front of her refrigerator. "You'll feel a whole lot better once you have something in your stomach."

Shifting Michelle higher, Susannah stood and followed him. "You can't just walk in here and—"

"I'll say I can't," he murmured, his head inside her fridge. "Do you realize there's nothing in here except an open box of soda and jar full of pickle juice?"

"I eat out a lot," Susannah said defensively.

"I can see that."

Michelle had finished the bottle and made a slurping sound that prompted Susannah to remove the nipple from her mouth. The baby's eyes were closed. Little wonder, Susannah thought. She was probably exhausted. Certainly Susannah was, and it was barely after seven Friday evening. And the weekend was only just beginning.

Setting the empty bottle on the kitchen counter, Susannah awkwardly lifted Michelle onto her shoulder and gently patted her back until she produced a tiny burp. Feeling a real sense of accomplishment, Susannah smiled proudly.

Nate chuckled and when Susannah glanced in his direction, she discovered him watching her, his grin warm and appraising. "You're going to be just fine."

Flustered, Susannah lowered her gaze. She always disliked it when a man looked at her that way, studying her features and forming a judgment about her by the size of her nose, or by the direction her eyebrows grew. Most men seemed to be of the opinion that they'd been granted a rare gift of insight and could determine a woman's entire character by just looking at her face. Unfortunately, Susannah's was too austere by conventional standards to be classified as beautiful. Her eyes were deep-set and dark, which had the effect of offsetting her high cheekbones. Her nose came almost straight from her forehead and together with her full mouth made her look like a classic Greek sculpture. Not pretty, she thought. Interesting perhaps.

It was during Susannah's beleaguered self-evaluation that Michelle stirred and started jabbering cheerfully, reaching one hand toward a strand of Susannah's dark hair.

Without her realizing it, her chignon had come undone. Michelle had somehow managed to loosen the pins and now the long dark tresses fell haphazardly over Susannah's shoulder. If there was one thing Susannah was meticulous about, and actually there were several, it was her appearance. She must look a rare sight, in a two-hundred-dollar business suit with a stained white blouse and her hair tumbling over her shoulder.

"Actually I've been waiting for an opportunity to introduce myself," Nate said, leaning against the counter, looking right at home. "But after the first couple of times we saw each other, our paths didn't seem to cross again."

"I've been working a lot of overtime lately." If the truth were known, Susannah almost always put in extra hours. Often she brought work home with her. She was dedicated, committed and hardworking. Her neighbor, however, didn't look as if he possessed any of those qualities. She strongly suspected that everything in life had come much too easily for Nate Townsend. She'd never seen him without his baseball cap or his T-shirt. Somehow she doubted he even owned a suit. Even if he did, it probably wouldn't look right on him. Nate Townsend was definitely a football-jersey type of guy.

He seemed likable enough, friendly and outgoing, but from what she'd seen, he lacked ambition. Apparently there had never been anything he'd wanted badly enough to really strive for.

"I'm glad we had the chance to introduce ourselves," Susannah added, walking back into the living room and toward her front door. "I appreciate the help, but as you said, Michelle and I are going to be just fine."

"Frankly, it didn't sound that way when I arrived."

"I was just getting my feet wet," she returned, defending herself, "and why are you arguing with me? You're the one who said I was doing all right."

"I lied."

"Why would you do that?"

Nate shrugged nonchalantly. "It was apparent a little self-confidence would do you a world of good, so I offered it."

Susannah glared at him, resenting his attitude. So much for the nice-guy-who-lives-next-door image she'd had of him up to this point. "I don't need any favors from you."

"You may not," he agreed, "but unfortunately Michelle does. The poor kid was starving and you didn't so much as suspect."

"I would have figured it out."

Nate gave her a look that seemed to cast doubt on her intelligence, and Susannah frowned right back. She opened the door with far more force than necessary and flipped her hair over her shoulder with flair a Paris model would have envied. "Thanks for stopping in," she said stiffly, "but as you can see everything's under control."

"If you say so." He gave her an off-center grin and without another word was gone.

Susannah banged the door shut with her hip, feeling a good deal of satisfaction as she did so. She realized this was petty, but her neighbor had irked her in more ways than one.

Soon afterward Susannah heard the soft strains of an Italian opera drifting from Nate's condominium. At least she thought it was Italian, which was unfortunate because it made her think of spaghetti and of how hungry she actually was.

"Okay, Michelle," she said, smiling down on her niece. "It's time to feed your auntie." Without too much trouble, Susannah assembled the high chair and set her niece in that while she scanned the contents of her freezer.

The best she could come up with was a frozen Mexican entrée. She gazed at the picture on the front of the package, shook her head and tossed it back inside the freezer.

Michelle seemed to approve and slapped her hands against the tray on her high chair.

Crossing her arms and leaning against the freezer door, Susannah paused. "Did you hear what he said?" she asked, still irate. "In a way he was right, but he didn't have to be so superior about it."

Michelle slapped her hands in approval once more. The vigorous strains of the music were muted by the thick walls, and wanting to hear a little more, Susannah cracked open the sliding glass door to her balcony, which was separated from Nate's by a concrete partition. It offered privacy, but didn't hold back the melodious voices raised in triumphant song.

Susannah opened the glass door completely and stepped outside. The evening was cool, but pleasantly so. The sun had just started to set and had cast a wash of golden shadows over the picturesque waterfront.

"Michelle," she muttered when she returned, "he's cooking something that smells like lasagna or spaghetti." Her stomach growled and she returned to the freezer, taking out the same Mexican entrée she'd rejected earlier. On second study, it didn't seem any more appetizing than the first time.

A faint scent of garlic wafted into her kitchen. Susannah turned her classic Greek nose in that direction, then followed the aroma to the open door like a puppet drawn there by a string. She sniffed loudly a couple of times and eagerly turned back to her niece. "It's definitely something Italian, and it smells divine."

Michelle pounded the tray again.

"It's garlic bread," Susannah announced and whirled around to face her niece, who appeared singularly unimpressed. But then, thought Susannah, she wouldn't be. She'd eaten.

Under normal conditions, Susannah would have reached for her jacket and headed to Mama Mataloni's, a fabulous Italian restaurant within easy walking distance. Unfortunately Mama Mataloni's didn't deliver.

Against her better judgment, Susannah stuck the frozen entrée into her microwave and set the timer. When her doorbell chimed, she stiffened and looked to Michelle as if the nine-month-old would sit up and tell Susannah who'd chosen to stop by this time.

It was Nate again, holding a plate of spaghetti and a small glass of red wine. "Did you fix yourself something to eat?" he asked.

For the life of her Susannah couldn't tear her gaze away from the oversize plate, heaped high with steaming pasta smothered in a thick red sauce. Nothing had ever looked more appetizing. He'd grated fresh Parmesan cheese over the top, which had melted onto the rich sauce. A generous slice of French bread was balanced on the side.

"I, ah, was just cooking up a... TV dinner." She pointed behind her toward the kitchen as if that would explain what she was trying to say. Her tongue seemed to be stuck to the roof of her mouth.

"I shouldn't have acted so superior earlier," he said, pushing the plate toward her. "I'm bringing you a peace offering."

"This... is for me?" She raised her eyes from the plate for the first time, wondering if he knew how hungry she felt and was toying with her.

He handed her the meal. "The sauce has been simmering most of the afternoon. I like to pretend I'm something of a gourmet chef. Every once in a while I get creative in the kitchen."

"How... nice." Her mind conjured up a picture of him standing in his kitchen stirring sauce while the rest of the world struggled to make a living. Her attitude wasn't the least bit gracious and she mentally apologized. Without further ado, she marched into her kitchen, reached for a fork and plopped herself down at the table. She might as well eat this feast while it was hot!

One sample told her everything she needed to know. "This is great." She took another bite, pointed her fork in his direction and rolled her eyes. "Marvelous. Wonderful."

Nate pulled a bread stick out of his shirt pocket and gave it to Michelle. "Here's looking at you, kid."

As Michelle chewed contentedly on the bread stick, Nate pulled out a chair and sat across from Susannah, who was too busy enjoying her dinner to notice anything out of the ordinary until Nate's gaze narrowed.

"Is something wrong?" Susannah asked. She wiped the edges of her mouth with a napkin and sampled the wine.

"I smell something."

From the look of him, whatever it was apparently wasn't pleasant. "It might be the TV dinner," she suggested hopefully, already knowing better.

"I'm afraid not."

Susannah straightened and carefully set the fork beside her plate as uneasiness settled over her.

"It seems," Nate said, sounding as if something was wrong with his nasal cavity, "that someone needs to change Michelle's diaper."

CHAPTER TWO

HOLDING A FRESHLY DIAPERED Michelle on her hip, Susannah rushed out of the bathroom into the narrow hallway and gasped for breath.

"Are you all right?" Nate asked, his brow creased with a concerned frown.

She nodded and sagged against the wall, feeling light-headed. Once she'd dragged several clean breaths through her lungs, she straightened and even managed a weak smile.

"It wasn't so bad now, was it?"

Susannah paused and glared at him. "I should have been wearing an oxygen mask."

Nate's responding chuckle did little to improve Susannah's mood.

"In light of what I just experienced," she said righteously, "I can't understand why the population continues to grow." To be on the safe side, she opened the hall linen closet and took out a large can of disinfectant spray. Sticking her arm inside the bathroom, she gave a generous squirt.

"While you were busy I assembled the crib," Nate told her, still revealing far too much amusement to suit Susannah. "Where would you like me to put it?"

"The living room will be fine." The gesture had been a thoughtful one, but Susannah wasn't accustomed to depending on others, so when she thanked him, the words were forced.

Susannah followed him into the living room and found the bed readied. She laid Michelle down on her stomach and covered her with a handmade blanket. The baby settled down immediately, without fussing.

Nate headed toward the door. "You're sure everything's going to be all right?" he said softly.

"Positive." Susannah wasn't, but Michelle was her niece and their problems weren't his. Nate had done more than enough already. "Thanks for dinner."

"Any time." He paused at the door and turned back. "I left my phone number on the kitchen counter. Call if you need me."

"Thanks."

He favored her with a grin on his way out the door, and Susannah stood a few moments after he'd vacated the apartment, thinking about him. Her feelings were decidedly mixed.

Susannah began sorting through the various bags her sister had left, depositing the jars of baby food in the cupboard and putting the bottles of formula in the fridge. As Nate had pointed out, there was plenty of room—all she had to do was scoot the empty pickle jar aside.

She supposed she should toss the jar in the garbage, but one of the guys from the office had mentioned something about pickling hard-boiled eggs. It sounded so simple—all she had to do was peel a few eggs and keep them refrigerated in the jar for a week or so. Susannah had been meaning to try the uncomplicated recipe ever since. But she feared that when the mood struck her, she wouldn't have any pickle juice around, so she kept it on hand just in case.

When she'd finished in the kitchen, Susannah soaked in a hot tub, leaving the door ajar in case Michelle woke and needed her. She felt worlds better afterward.

Walking on the tips of her toes back into the living room, she brought out her briefcase and removed a fat file. She paused and glanced down at her sleeping niece and gently patted her back. The little girl looked so angelic, so content.

Suddenly a powerful yearning stirred within Susannah, one she wasn't sure she could put a name to. She felt real affection for Michelle, but the feeling was more than that. This time alone with her niece had evoked a longing buried deep in Susannah's heart, a longing she had never taken the time to fully examine. And with it came an aching restless sensation that she promptly submerged.

When Susannah had chosen a career in business, she'd realized she was giving up the part of herself that hungered for husband and children. There was nothing that said she couldn't marry, couldn't raise a child, but she knew herself too well. From the time she was in high school it had been painfully apparent she was completely inadequate in the domestic arena. Especially when she compared herself to Emily, who seemed to have been born with a dust rag in one hand and a cookbook in the other.

Susannah had never regretted the decision she'd made to dedicate herself to her career, but then she was more fortunate than others. She had Emily, who was determined to supply her with numerous nieces and nephews. For Susannah, Michelle and the little ones who were sure to follow would have to be enough.

Comfortable with herself and her choices, Susannah quietly stepped away from the crib. For the next hour, she sat on her mattress reading the details of the proposed marketing program the department had sent her. Their full presentation would follow on Monday morning and she wanted to be informed and prepared.

When she finished reading the report, she tiptoed back to her desk, situated in the far corner of the living room, and replaced the file in her briefcase.

Once more she paused to check on her niece. Feeling just a little cocky, she returned to the bedroom convinced this baby-sitting business wasn't going to be so bad after all.

SUSANNAH CHANGED her mind at one-thirty when a piercing wail startled her out of a sound sleep. Not knowing how long Michelle had been at it, Susannah nearly fell out of bed in her rush to reach her niece.

"Michelle," she cried, blindly stumbling across the floor, her arms stretched out in front of her. "I'm coming.... There's no need to panic."

Michelle disagreed vehemently.

Turning on a light only made matters worse. Squinting to protect her eyes from the glare, Susannah groped her way to the crib, then let out a cry herself when she stubbed her toe on the leg of the coffee table.

Michelle was standing, holding on to the bars and looking as if she didn't have a friend in the world.

"What's the matter, sweetheart?" Susannah asked softly, lifting the little one into her arms.

A wet bottom told part of the story, but also the poor tyke had probably woken and, finding herself in a strange place, felt scared. Susannah couldn't blame her.

"All right, we'll try this diapering business a second time."

Susannah spread a thick towel on the bathroom counter, then gently placed Michelle on it. She was halfway through the changing process when the phone pealed. Straightening, Susannah glanced around her, wondering what she should do. She couldn't leave Michelle, and picking her up and carting her into the kitchen would be difficult. Whoever was calling at this time of night should know better! If it was important they could leave a message on her answering machine.

But after three rings, the phone stopped, followed almost immediately by a firm knock against her front door.

Hauling Michelle, freshly powdered and diapered, with her, Susannah squinted and checked the peephole to discover a disgruntled Nate on the other side.

"Nate," she said in surprise as she opened the door. She couldn't even guess what he wanted. And she wasn't too keen about letting him inside her apartment at this hour.

He stood just inside the condo, barefoot and dressed in a red plaid housecoat. His hair was mussed as if he'd recently woken, which made Susannah wonder about her own disheveled appearance. She feared she looked like someone who'd walked out of a swamp.

"Is Michelle all right?" he barked, despite the evidence before him. Not waiting for a reply, he continued in an accusing tone, "You didn't answer the phone."

"I couldn't. I was changing her diaper."

Nate hesitated and then studied her closely. "In that case, are you all right?"

She nodded and managed to raise her right hand. It was difficult when her arms were occupied with a baby. "I lived to tell about it."

"Good. What happened? Why was Michelle crying?"

"I'm not sure. Maybe when she woke up and didn't recognize her surroundings, she suffered an anxiety attack."

"And, from the look of us, caused a couple more."

Susannah didn't want to look at herself. Her mussed and knotted hair spilled over her shoulder like an oil slick. She too was barefoot. She'd been so anxious to get to Michelle that she hadn't taken the time to reach for her slippers or her robe.

Michelle, it seemed, was pleased with all the unexpected attention, and when she leaned toward Nate, arms outstretched, Susannah marveled at how fickle an infant could be. After all, she was the one who had fed and diapered her. Not Nate.

"It's my male charm," he explained, looking delighted.

"More likely, it's your red housecoat."

Whatever it was, Michelle went into his arms as if he was a long-lost friend. Susannah excused herself to retrieve her robe from the foot of her bed. By the time she returned, Nate was sitting on the sofa with his feet stretched out in front of him, supported by Susannah's mahogany coffee table.

"Make yourself at home," she muttered. Her mood wasn't always the best when she'd been startled out of a sound sleep.

He glanced up at her and grinned. "There's no need to be testy."

"Yes, there is," she countered and destroyed what remained of her argument by yawning loudly. Covering her mouth with the back of her hand, she slumped down on the chair across from him and flipped her hair away from her face.

His gaze followed the action. "You should wear your hair down more often."

She glared at him once more, fuming. "I always wear my hair up."

"I noticed. And frankly, it's much more flattering down."

"Oh, for heaven's sake," she cried, "are you going to tell me how to dress next?"

"I might."

He said it with such a charming smile that any sting there might have been in his statement was diluted.

"There's no need to stick with business suits every day, is there? Try a dress sometime—a frilly thing with lace and buttons."

She opened her mouth to argue with him, then decided it wouldn't do any good. The arrogance he displayed seemed to be characteristic of handsome men in general, she'd noted. Because a man happened to possess lean good looks and could smile beguilingly, he figured he had the right to say anything he pleased to a woman. As if it was up to him to comment on how she styled her hair, how she chose to dress or anything else. These were things he wouldn't dream of suggesting if he were talking to another man.

"You aren't going to argue?"

"No," she said, and for emphasis shook her head.

That stopped him short. He paused and blinked, then gave her another of his captivating smiles. "I find that refreshing."

"I'm gratified to hear there's something about me you approve of." There were probably several other things about her that didn't please him. Given any encouragement, he would probably be glad to list them for her.

Sweet little traitor that she was, Michelle had curled up in Nate's arms, utterly content just to sit there and study his handsome face, which no doubt had fascinated numerous other females before her. The least Michelle could do was show some signs of going back to sleep so Susannah could return her to the crib and usher Nate out the door.

"I shouldn't have said what I did about your hair and clothes."

"Hey," she returned flippantly, "you don't need to worry about hurting my feelings. I've got a lot of emotional fortitude."

"Strong," he repeated. "You make yourself sound like an all-weather tire."

"I've had to be a good deal tougher than that."

His face relaxed into a look of sympathy. "Why?"

"I work with men just like you every day."

"Men just like me?"

"It's true. For the past seven years, I've found myself up against the old double standard, but I've learned to keep my cool."

He frowned as if he didn't understand what she was talking about. Susannah felt it was her obligation to tell him. Apparently Nate had never been involved in office politics. "Let me give you a few examples. If a male co-worker has a cluttered desk, then everyone assumes he's a hard worker. If my desk is a mess, it's a sign of disorganization."

Nate straightened and looked as if he wanted to argue with her, but Susannah was just warming to her subject and she continued before he had a chance to speak. "If a man in an office marries, it's good for the

company because he'll settle down and become a more
productive employee. If a woman marries, it's almost
the kiss of death because management figures she'll get
pregnant and leave. She's the last one to be offered a
promotion no matter how qualified she is. If a man
leaves because he's been offered a better job, everyone's pleased for him because he's taking advantage of
an excellent career opportunity. But if the same position is offered to a woman and she takes it, then upper
management shrugs and claims women aren't depend-
able anyway."

When she'd finished there was a short pause. "You
certainly have strong feelings on the subject," he said
at last.

"If you were a woman, you would, too."

His nod of agreement was a long time coming.
"You're right, I probably would."

Michelle seemed to find the toes of her sleeper fasci-
nating and was examining them with sheer delight.
Personally, Susannah didn't know how anyone could
look so wide-awake at this ungodly hour.

"If you turn down the lights, she might get the hint,"
Nate said, doing a poor job of smothering a yawn.

"You look beat," said Susannah. "There's no need
for you to stay. I'll take her." She held out her arms to
Michelle, who whimpered and clung all the more tightly
to Nate. Susannah's feelings of inadequacy were reinforced.

"Don't worry about me. I'm comfortable," Nate told
her.

"But . . ." She could feel the warmth invading her
cheeks. She lowered her gaze, regretting her outburst of
a few minutes ago. She'd been standing on her soap-
box again. "Listen, I'm sorry about what I said. What

goes on at the office has nothing to do with our being neighbors.''

"Then we're even."

"Even?"

"I shouldn't have commented on your hair and clothes." He hesitated long enough to envelop her in his smile. "Friends?"

Despite the intolerable hour, Susannah found herself smiling back. "Friends."

Michelle seemed to concur because she cooed loudly, kicking her feet.

Susannah stood and turned the lamp down to its lowest setting, then reached for Michelle's blanket, covering the baby with that. Feeling slightly chilled herself, she retrieved the brightly colored afghan at the foot of the sofa, which Emily had crocheted for her last Christmas.

The muted light created an intimate atmosphere, and suddenly self-conscious, Susannah suggested, "Maybe if I sing to her. That should help her go to sleep."

"If anyone sings, it'll be me," he said much too quickly.

Susannah's pride was a little dented, but remembering her limited repertoire of songs, she gestured toward him and said, "All right, Frank Sinatra, have a go."

To Susannah's surprise, Nate's singing voice was soothing and melodious. More amazingly, he knew exactly the right kind of tunes to sing. Not baby songs, but easy-listening ones, the kind she'd heard for years on the radio. She felt her own eyes drifting closed and battled to stay awake. His voice dropped to a mere whisper that felt like a warm caress. Much too warm. And cozy, as if the three of them belonged together, which was ridiculous since she'd only just met Nate. He was her neighbor and nothing more. There hadn't been time for them to get to know each other, and Michelle was her *niece*, not her daughter.

But the domestic fantasy continued no matter how hard she tried to dispel it. She couldn't stop thinking about what it would be like to share her life with a husband and children—and also manage to keep her eyes open for more than a second or two. Perhaps if she rested them for just a moment...

THE NEXT THING Susannah knew her neck ached. She reached up to secure her pillow, then realized she didn't have one. Instead of being in her bed, she was curled up in the chair, her head resting uncomfortably against the arm. Slowly, reluctantly, she opened her eyes and discovered Nate sitting across from her, his head tilted back, sleeping soundly. Michelle was resting peacefully in his arms.

It took Susannah a moment to orient herself. When she realized the sun was breaking across the sky and spilling into her large windows, she closed her eyes again. It was morning. Morning! Nate had spent the night in her condominium.

Flustered, Susannah twisted her body into an upright position and rubbed the sleep from her face, wondering what she should do. Waking Nate was probably not the best idea. He was bound to be as unnerved as she to discover he'd fallen asleep in her living room. To complicate matters, the afghan she'd covered herself with had somehow become twisted around her legs and hips. Muttering under her breath, Susannah yanked it about in an effort to stand.

Her activity disturbed Nate's restful slumber. He stirred, glanced in her direction and then froze for what seemed the longest moment of Susannah's life. Then he blinked several times and glared at her as if he felt certain she'd vanish into thin air provided he looked at her long enough.

Standing now, Susannah did her best to appear dignified, which was nearly impossible with the comforter still twisted around her hips and legs like a coiled rope.

"Where am I?" Nate asked dazedly.

"Ah . . . my place."

His eyes drifted shut. "I was afraid of that." The mournful look that came over Nate's face would have been comical under other circumstances. Only neither of them was laughing.

"I, ah, must have fallen asleep," she said, breaking the embarrassed silence. She took pains to fold the afghan, and then held it against her stomach like a shield.

"Me too, apparently," Nate muttered.

Michelle woke and struggled into a sitting position. She looked around her and evidently didn't like what she saw, either. Her lower lip started to tremble.

"Michelle, it's okay," Susannah said quickly, hoping to ward off the jungle yell she feared was coming. "You're staying with Auntie Susannah this weekend, remember?"

"I think she might be wet," Nate offered when Michelle started to whimper softly. He let out a muffled curse and hastily lifted the nine-month-old from his lap. "I'm positive she's wet. Here, take her."

Susannah reached for her niece and a dry diaper in one smooth movement, but it did little good. Michelle was intent on letting them both know, in no uncertain terms, that she didn't like her schedule altered. Nor did she appreciate waking up in a stranger's arms. She conveyed her displeasure in loud boisterous cries.

"I think she might be hungry, too," Nate suggested, trying to brush the dampness from his housecoat.

"Brilliant observation," Susannah said sarcastically on her way to the bathroom, Michelle in her arms.

"My, my, you certainly get testy in the mornings," he said.

"I need coffee."

"Fine. I'll make us both a cup while I'm heating a bottle for Michelle."

"She's supposed to eat her cereal first," Susannah shouted. At least that was what Emily had insisted when she outlined her daughter's schedule.

"I don't think she cares. She's hungry."

"All right, all right," Susannah yelled from the bathroom. "Heat her bottle first if you want."

Yelling was a mistake, she soon discovered. Michelle apparently wasn't any keener on mornings than Susannah was. Punching the air with her stubby legs, her niece made diapering nearly an impossible task. Susannah grew more frustrated by the minute. Finally her hair, falling forward over her shoulders, caught Michelle's attention. She grasped it, pausing long enough to suck in a huge breath.

"Do you want me to get that?" she heard Nate shout.

"Get what?"

Apparently it wasn't important because he didn't answer her. But a moment or so later he was standing at the bathroom door.

"It's for you," he said.

"What's for me?"

"The phone."

The word bounced off the walls of her mind like a ricocheting bullet. "Did ... did they say who it was?"

she asked, her voice high-pitched and wobbly. No doubt it was someone from the office and she would be the subject of gossip for months.

"Someone named Emily."

"Emily," she repeated. That was even worse. Her sister was sure to be full of awkward questions.

"Hi," Susannah said as casually as possible into the receiver.

"Who answered the phone?" her sister demanded without preamble.

"My neighbor, Nate Townsend. He, ah, lives next door." The finesse with which she delivered that brilliant explanation amazed even her. Worse, Susannah had been ready to blurt out that Nate had spent the night, but she'd stopped herself just in time.

"I haven't met him, have I?"

"My neighbor? No, you haven't."

"He sounds cute."

"Listen, if you're phoning about Michelle," Susannah hurried to add, anxious to end the conversation, "there's no need for concern. Everything's under control." That was a slight exaggeration, but what Emily didn't know couldn't worry her.

"Is that Michelle I hear crying in the background?" Emily asked, sounding concerned.

"Yes. She just woke up and she's a little hungry." Nate was holding the baby and pacing the kitchen, impatiently waiting for Susannah to get off the phone.

"My poor baby," Emily said. "Tell me when you met your neighbor. I don't remember you ever mentioning anyone named Nate."

"He's been helping me out," Susannah said quickly. Wanting to change the subject, she asked, "How are you and Robert?"

Her sister sighed audibly. "Robert was so right. We needed this time alone. I feel a thousand times better and so does he. Every married couple should get away for a few days like this, but then everyone doesn't have a sister as generous as you to fill in on such short notice."

"Good, good," Susannah said, hardly aware of what she was supposed to think was so fantastic. "Uh-oh," she said, growing desperate. "Michelle's bottle is warm. I hate to cut you off, sis, but I've got to go take care of Michelle. I'm sure you understand."

"Of course."

"I'll see you tomorrow afternoon then. What time's your flight landing?"

"One-fifteen. We'll drive straight to your place and pick up Michelle."

"Okay, I'll expect you sometime around two then." Another day with Michelle. She could manage for an additional twenty-four hours, couldn't she? What could possibly go wrong in that small amount of time?

Losing patience, Nate took the bottle and Michelle and returned to the living room. Susannah watched through the doorway as he turned on her television set and plopped himself down as if he'd been doing it for years. His concentration moved from the TV long enough to place the rubber nipple in Michelle's eager mouth.

Her niece began greedily sucking, too hungry to care who was feeding her. Good heavens, Susannah thought,

Michelle had spent the night in his arms. A little thing like letting this man feed her paled in comparison.

Emily continued chatting, telling her sister how romantic her first night in San Francisco had been. But Susannah barely heard. Her gaze settled on Nate, who looked rumpled, crumpled and utterly content, sitting in her living room, holding an infant in his arms.

The sight affected Susannah as few ever had, and she was powerless to explain its impact on her senses. She'd dated a good number of men—debonair, rich, sophisticated ones. But the feeling she had now, this attraction, had taken her completely by surprise. Over the years, despite her dates, Susannah had always been careful to guard her heart. It hadn't been difficult, since she'd never met anyone who truly appealed to her. Yet this disheveled, disgruntled male, who sat in her living room holding and feeding her infant niece with enviable expertise, attracted her more profoundly than anyone she'd ever met. It didn't make the least bit of sense. Nothing could ever develop between them—they were as different as gelatin and concrete. The last thing she wanted was to become involved in a serious relationship. With some effort, she forced her eyes away from the homey scene.

When at last she was able to hang up the phone, Susannah moved into the living room, feeling almost weary. She brushed the tangled curls from her face, wondering if she should take Michelle from Nate so he could return to his own apartment. No doubt her niece would resist and humiliate her once more.

"Your sister isn't flying with Puget Air, is she?" he asked, frowning. His gaze remained on the television screen.

"Yes, why?"

Nate's mouth thinned. "You...we're in trouble here. Big trouble. According to the news, maintenance workers for Puget Air are going on strike. By six tonight, every plane they own will be grounded."

CHAPTER THREE

"IF THIS IS A JOKE," Susannah told him angrily, "it's in poor taste."

"Would I kid about something like this?" Nate demanded.

Susannah slumped down on the edge of the cushion and gave a ragged sigh. This couldn't be happening to her, it just couldn't. "I'd better call Emily." She assumed her sister was blissfully unaware of the strike.

Susannah returned a few minutes later.

"Well," Nate demanded, "what did she say?"

"Oh, she knew all along," Susannah replied disparagingly, "but she didn't want to say anything because she was afraid I'd worry."

"How exactly does she intend to get back to Seattle?"

"Apparently they booked passage on another airline on the off chance something like this might happen."

"That was smart."

"My brother-in-law is like that. I'm not to give the matter another thought," she said, quoting Emily. "My sister will be back Sunday afternoon as promised." If the fates so decreed, and Susannah said a fervent prayer they would.

But the fates had other plans.

SUNDAY MORNING, there were bags under Susannah's eyes. She was exhausted mentally and physically, and convinced anew that motherhood was definitely not for her. Two nights into the ordeal, Susannah had noted that the emotional stirring for a husband and children came to her only when Michelle was sleeping or eating. And with good reason.

Nate arrived around nine bearing gifts. He brought freshly baked cinnamon rolls still warm from the oven. He stood in her doorway, tall and lean, with a smile bright enough to dazzle the most dedicated career woman. Once more, Susannah was amazed at her overwhelming reaction to him. Her heart leaped to her throat, and she immediately wished she'd taken time to dress in something better than her faded housecoat.

"You look terrible."

"Thanks," she said, bouncing Michelle on her hip.

"I take it you had a bad night."

"Michelle was fussing. New tooth coming in. She didn't seem the least bit interested in sleeping." She wiped a hand over her face, certain she'd never looked worse.

"I wish you'd called me," Nate said, taking her by the elbow and leading her into the kitchen. He actually looked guilty because he'd had a peaceful night's rest. Ridiculous, Susannah thought.

"Call you? Whatever for?" she asked. "So you could have paced with her, too?" As it was, Nate had spent a good portion of Saturday in and out of her apartment helping her. Spending a second night with them was above and beyond the call of duty. "Did I tell you," Susannah said, yawning, "Michelle's got a new tooth coming in—I felt it myself." Deposited in the high chair, Michelle was content for the moment.

Nate nodded and glanced at his watch. "What time does your sister's flight arrive?"

"One-fifteen." No sooner had the words left her lips when the phone rang. Susannah's and Nate's eyes locked, and as it rang a second time she wondered how a telephone could sound so much like a death knell. Even before she answered it, Susannah knew it was what she'd most dreaded hearing.

"Well?" Nate asked when she'd finished.

Covering her face with both hands, Susannah sagged against the wall.

"Say something," Nate demanded.

Slowly she lowered her hands. "Help."

"Help?"

"Yes," she cried, struggling to keep her voice from cracking. "All Puget Air flights are grounded just the way the news reported they would be, and the other airline Robert and Emily made reservations with is overbooked. The earliest flight they can take is tomorrow morning."

"I see."

"Obviously you don't!" she cried. "Tomorrow is Monday and I've got to be at work!"

"Call in sick."

"I can't do that," she snapped, angry with him for even suggesting such a thing. "Marketing is giving their presentation and I've got to be there."

"Why?"

She glared at him. It was futile to expect someone like Nate to understand something as important as a sales presentation. Nate didn't seem to have a job; he didn't worry about a career. For that matter he couldn't possibly grasp that a woman holding a management position had to strive twice as hard to prove herself.

"I'm not trying to be cute, Susannah," he said with infuriating calm. "I honestly want to know why that meeting is so important."

"Because it is. I don't expect you to appreciate something like this, so just accept the fact that I *have* to be there."

Nate cocked his head and idly rubbed the side of his jaw. "First, answer me something. Five years from now, will this meeting make a difference in your life?"

"I don't know." She pressed two fingers to the bridge of her nose. She'd had less than three hours' sleep, and Nate was asking impossible questions. Michelle, bless her devilish little heart, had fallen asleep in her high chair. Why shouldn't she? Susannah reasoned. She'd spent the entire night fussing, and was exhausted now. By the time Susannah had discovered the new tooth, she felt as if she'd grown it herself.

"If I were you, I wouldn't sweat it," Nate said with that same nonchalant attitude. "If you aren't there to hear their presentation, marketing will give it Tuesday morning."

"In other words," she muttered, "you're saying I don't have a thing to worry about."

"Exactly."

Nate Townsend knew next to nothing about surviving in the corporate world, and he'd obviously been protected from life's harsher realities. It was all too obvious to Susannah that he was a man with a baseball-cap mentality. He couldn't be expected to fully comprehend her dilemma.

"So," he said now, "what are you going to do?"

Susannah wasn't entirely sure. Briefly, she closed her eyes in an effort to concentrate. *Impose discipline,* she said to herself. *Stay calm,* that was important above all else. *Think slowly and analyze your objectives.* For every problem there was a solution.

"Susannah?"

She glanced at him; she'd almost forgotten he was with her. "I'll cancel my early-morning appointments and go in for the presentation," she stated matter-of-factly, having arrived at a manageable decision.

"What about Michelle? Are you going to hire a sitter?"

A baby-sitter hired by the baby-sitter. A novel thought, perhaps even viable, but Susannah didn't know anyone who sat with babies.

Then she made her decision. She would take Michelle to work with her.

And that was exactly what she did.

As she knew it would, Susannah's arrival at H&J Lima caused quite a stir. At precisely ten the following morning, she stepped off the elevator. Her black eelskin briefcase was clenched in one hand and Michelle was pressed against her hip with the other. Head held high, Susannah marched across the hardwood floor, past the long rows of doorless cubicles and shelves of foot-thick file binders. Several employees moved away from their desks to view her progress. A low rumble of hushed whispers followed her.

"Good morning, Ms Brooks," Susannah said crisply as she walked into her office, the diaper bag draped over her shoulder like an ammunition pouch.

"Ms Simmons."

Susannah noted that her secretary, to her credit, didn't so much as bat an eye. The woman was well trained; to all outward appearances, Susannah regularly arrived at the office with a nine-month-old infant attached to her hip.

Depositing the diaper bag on the floor, Susannah took her place behind a six-foot-wide walnut desk. Content for the moment, Michelle sat on her lap, gleefully viewing her aunt's domain.

"Would you like some coffee?" Ms Brooks asked.

"Yes, please."

Her secretary paused. "Will your, ah..."

"This is my niece, Michelle, Ms Brooks."

The woman nodded. "Will Michelle require anything to drink?"

"No, thanks anyway. Is there anything urgent in the mail?"

"Nothing that can't wait. I canceled your eight and nine o'clock appointments," her secretary went on to explain. "When I spoke to Mr. Adams, he asked if you could join him for drinks tomorrow night at six."

"That'll be fine." The old lecher would love to do all their business outside the office. This time, she'd agree to his terms, since she'd been the one to cancel the appointment, but she wouldn't be so willing a second time. She'd never much cared for Andrew Adams, who was overweight, balding and a general nuisance.

"Will you be needing me for anything else?" her secretary asked when she delivered the coffee.

"Nothing. Thank you."

As she should have predicted, the meeting with marketing was an unmitigated disaster. The presentation took twenty-two minutes, and in that short time Michelle managed to dismantle Susannah's Cross pen, unfasten her blouse and pull her hair free from her carefully styled French twist. Several times the baby had clapped her hands and made loud noises. At the low point of the meeting, Susannah had been forced to leave her seat and crawl under her desk to retrieve her niece, who was cheerfully crawling over everyone's feet.

By the time she arrived back at her condo, Susannah felt as if she were returning from a war zone. It was the type of day that made her crave something chocolate and excessively sweet. But there weren't enough chocolate chip cookies in the world to see her through another morning like that one.

To Susannah's surprise, Nate met her in the foyer outside the elevator. She took one look at him and resisted the urge to burst into tears.

"I take it things didn't go well."

"How'd you guess?" she questioned sarcastically.

"It might be the fact you're wearing your hair down when I specifically remember you left wearing it up. Or it could be that your blouse is buttoned wrong and there's a gaping hole in the middle." His smile was devilish. "I wondered if you were the type to wear a lacy bra. Now I know."

Susannah groaned and slapped a hand over her front. He could have spared her that comment.

"Here, kiddo," he said, taking Michelle out of Susannah's arms. "It looks like we need to give your poor aunt a break."

Turning her back, Susannah refastened her blouse and then brought out her key. Her once orderly, immaculate apartment looked as if a cyclone had gone through it. Blankets and baby toys were scattered from one end of the living room the other. She'd slept on the couch in order to be close to Michelle, and her pillow and blankets were still there along with her blue suit jacket, which she'd been forced to change when Michelle had tossed a spoonful of plums on the sleeve.

"What happened here?" Nate asked, looking in astonishment at the scene before him.

"Three days and three nights with Michelle and you need to ask?"

"Sit down," he said gently. "I'll get you a cup of coffee." Susannah did as he suggested, too grateful to argue with him.

Nate stopped just inside the kitchen. "What's this purple stuff all over the walls?"

"Plums," Susannah informed him. "I discovered the hard way that Michelle hates plums."

The scene in the kitchen was a good example of how her morning had gone. It had taken Susannah the better part of three hours to get herself and Michelle ready for the excursion to the office. And that was just the beginning.

"What I need is a double martini," she told Nate when he carried in two cups of coffee.

"It's not even noon."

"I know," she said, slowly lowering herself onto the sofa. "Can you imagine what I'd require if it was two o'clock?"

Chuckling, Nate handed her the steaming cup. Michelle was sitting on the carpet, content to play with the very toys she'd vehemently rejected that morning.

To Susannah's surprise, Nate sat down next to her and looped his arm over her shoulder. She tensed, but if he noticed, he chose to ignore it. He stretched his legs out on top of the coffee table and relaxed.

Susannah felt her tension mount. The memory of the meeting with marketing was enough to elevate her blood pressure, but when she analyzed this strained tautness, she realized it came from being so close to Nate. It wasn't that Susannah objected to his touch; in fact quite the opposite was true. They'd spent three days in close quarters, and contrary to everything she'd theorized about her neighbor, she had come to appreciate his happy-go-lucky approach to life. But it was diametrically opposed to her own view, and the fact that she could be so attracted to him was something of a shock.

"Do you want to talk about marketing's presentation?"

She released her breath slowly. "No, I think this morning is best forgotten by everyone involved. You were right, I should have postponed the meeting."

Nate sipped his coffee and said, "It's one of those live-and-learn situations."

Pulling herself to a standing position at the coffee table, Michelle cheerfully edged her way around until she was stopped by Nate's outstretched legs. Then she surprised them both by reaching out one arm and granting him a smile that would have melted concrete.

"Oh, look," Susannah cried proudly, "you can see her new tooth!"

"Where?" Lifting the baby onto his lap, Nate peered inside her mouth. Susannah was trying to show him where to look when the doorbell chimed in three impatient bursts.

When Susannah answered the door, Emily flew in as if she had suddenly sprouted wings. "My baby," she cried. "Mommy missed you so-o-o much."

Not half as much as I missed you, Emily, she mused, watching the happy reunion.

Robert followed on his wife's heels, looking pleased. The weekend away had apparently done them both a world of good. Never mind that it had nearly destroyed Susannah's peace of mind and her business career.

"You must be Nate," Emily said, claiming the seat beside Susannah's neighbor. "My sister couldn't say enough about you."

· "Coffee anyone?" Susannah piped up eagerly, rubbing her palms together. The last thing she needed was her sister applying her matchmaking techniques to her and Nate. Emily strongly believed it was unnatural for Susannah to live the way she did. A career was one thing, but choosing to forgo the personal satisfaction of a husband and family was beyond her sister's comprehension. Being fulfilled in that role herself, Emily assumed that Susannah was missing an essential part of life.

"Nothing for me," Robert answered.

"In fact, I bet you're eager to pack up everything and head home," Susannah stated hopefully. Her eye happened to catch Nate's, and it was obvious he was struggling not to laugh at her less-than-subtle attempt to usher her sister and family on their way.

"Susannah's right," Robert said, glancing around the room. It was clear he'd never seen his orderly, efficient sister-in-law's home in such a state of disarray.

"But I've hardly had a chance to talk to Nate," Emily protested. "And I was looking forward to getting to know him better."

"I'll be around," Nate said lightly.

His gaze settled on Susannah, and the look he gave her caused her insides to quiver. For the first time she realized how much she wanted this man to kiss her. Susannah wasn't the type of person who looked at a handsome male and wondered how his mouth would feel on hers. She was convinced this current phenomenon had a good deal to do with sheer exhaustion, but whatever the cause she found her eyes riveted to his.

Emily suddenly noticed what was happening. "Yes, I think you may be right, Robert," she said, and her voice contained more than a hint of amusement. "I'll pack Michelle's things."

Susannah's cheeks were pink with embarrassment by the time she tore her gaze away from Nate's. "By the way, did you know Michelle has an aversion to plums?"

"I can't say that I did," Emily said, busily throwing her daughter's things together.

Nate helped disassemble the crib and the high chair, and it seemed no more than a few minutes had passed when Susannah's condo was once more her own. She stood in the middle of the living room savoring the silence. It was pure bliss.

"They're off," she said when she realized Nate had stayed behind.

"Like a herd of turtles."

Susannah had heard that saying from the time she was a kid. She didn't find it particularly funny anymore, but she shared a smile with him.

"I have my life back now," she sighed. It would probably take her the better part of a month to recover, though.

"Your life is your own," Nate agreed, watching her closely.

Susannah would have liked to attribute the tears that flooded her eyes to his close scrutiny, but she knew better. With her hands cradling her middle, she walked over to the window, which looked out over Elliott Bay. A green-and-white ferry glided peacefully over the darker green waters. Rain tapped gently against the window, and the sky, a deep oyster-gray, promised drizzle for most of the afternoon.

Hoping Nate wouldn't notice, she wiped the tears from her face and drew in a deep calming breath.

"Susannah?"

"I . . . I was just looking at the Sound. It's so lovely this time of year." She could hear him approach her from behind, and when he placed his hands on her shoulders it was all she could do to keep from leaning against him and absorbing his strength.

"You're crying."

She nodded, sniffling because it was impossible to hold it inside any longer.

"It's not like you to cry, is it? What's wrong?"

"I don't know . . ." she said and hiccuped on a sob. "I can't believe I'm doing this. I love that little tyke . . . we were just beginning to understand each other . . . and . . . dear heaven, I'm glad Emily came back when . . . she did." Before Susannah realized how much she was missing without a husband and family.

Nate ran his hands down her arms in the gentlest of caresses.

He didn't say anything for a long time, and Susannah was convinced she was making an absolute idiot of herself. Nate was right. It wasn't like her to dissolve into tears. This unexpected burst of emotion must have been a result of the trauma she'd experienced that morning in her office, or the fact she hadn't had a decent night's sleep in what felt like a month and, yes, she'd admit it, of her having met Nate.

Without saying another word, Nate turned her around and lifted her chin with his finger, raising her eyes to his. His look was so tender, so caring, that Susannah sniffled again. Her shoulders shook and she wiped at her nose.

He brushed away the hair that clung to the side of her damp face. His fingertips slowly slid over each of her features as though he were a blind man trying to memorize her face. Susannah was mesmerized, unable to pull away. Slowly, as if denying himself the pleasure for as long as he could, he lowered his mouth.

When his lips settled on hers, Susannah released a long, barely audible sigh. She'd wondered earlier what it would be like when Nate kissed her. Now she knew. His kiss was soft and warm. Velvet smooth, and infinitely gentle, yet somehow electric.

As if one sample wasn't enough, he kissed her again. This time it was Nate who sighed. Then he dropped his hands and stepped back.

Startled by the abrupt action, Susannah swayed slightly. Nate's arms righted her. Apparently he'd come to his senses about the same time as she had. For a brief moment they'd decided to ignore their differences. The only thing they had in common was the fact they lived in the same building, she reminded herself. Their values and expectations were worlds apart.

"Are you all right?" he asked, frowning.

She blinked a couple of times, trying to find a way to disguise that she wasn't. Everything had happened much too fast; her heart was galloping like a runaway horse. She'd never been so attracted to a man in her life. "Of course I'm all right," she said with strained bravado. "Are you?"

He didn't answer for a long moment. Instead he stuffed his hands in his pants pocket and moved away from her, looking annoyed.

"Nate?" she whispered.

He paused long enough to scowl in her direction. Rubbing his hand across his brow, he twisted the ever-present baseball cap backward as if he were catcher. "I think we should try that again."

Susannah wasn't sure what he meant until he reached for her. His first few kisses had been gentle, but this one was meant to take charge of her senses. His mouth moved over hers until she felt the starch go out of her knees. In an effort to maintain her balance, she gripped his shoulders, and although she fought it, she quickly surrendered to the swirling excitement. Nate's kiss was debilitating. She couldn't breathe, couldn't think, couldn't move.

Nate groaned, then his grip tightened and shifted to the back of her head. He slanted his mouth over hers, and moved his lips as if he were playing an intricate musical instrument. At length he released a jagged breath and buried his face in the soft curve of her neck. "What about now?"

"You're a good kisser."

"That's not what I meant, Susannah. You feel it too, don't you? You must! There's enough electricity between us to light up a city block."

"No," she lied, and swallowed tightly. "It was nice as far as kisses go—"

"Nice!"

"Very nice," she amended, hoping to appease him, "but that's about it."

Nate didn't say anything for a long minute, a painfully long minute. Then, scowling at her, he turned and walked out of her apartment.

Trembling, Susannah watched him go. His kiss had touched a chord within her, notes that had been long-silent deep within her, and now she feared the music would forever mark her soul. But she couldn't let him know that. They had nothing in common. They were mismatched.

NOW THAT SHE WAS SEATED in the plush cocktail lounge with her associate, Andrew Adams, Susannah regretted having agreed to meet him after hours. It was apparent from the moment she stepped into the dimly lit room that he had more on his mind than discussing business. Despite the fact that Adams was balding and overweight, he would have been appealing enough if he hadn't looked upon himself as some kind of modern-day Adonis. Although Susannah struggled to maintain a business-like calm, it was becoming increasingly difficult, and she wondered how much longer her good intentions would hold.

"There are some figures I meant to show you," Adams said holding the stem of his martini glass with both hands and studying Susannah with undisguised admiration. "Unfortunately I left them at my apartment. Why don't we conclude our talk there?"

Susannah made a point of looking at her watch and frowning, hoping her associate would take the hint. Something told her differently. "I'm afraid I won't have the time," she said. It was almost seven and she'd already spent an hour with him.

"My place is only a few blocks from here," he coaxed.

His look was much too suggestive, and Susannah was growing wearier by the minute. As far as she could see, this entire evening had been a waste of valuable time.

The only thing that interested her was returning to her own place and talking to Nate. He'd been on her mind all day and she was eager to see him again. The truth was that she was downright nervous after their last meeting, and wondered how they'd react to each other now. Nate had left her so abruptly, and she hadn't talked to him since.

"John Hammer and I are good friends," Adams claimed, pulling his chair closer to her own. "I don't know if you're aware of that."

He didn't even bother to veil his threat. Susannah worked directly under John Hammer, who would have the final say on the appointment of vice president. Susannah and two others were in the running for the position. And Susannah wanted it. Badly. She could achieve her five-year goal if she got it, and in the process make H&J Lima history—by being the first female vice president.

"If you're such good friends with Mr. Hammer," she said, doing an admirable job of keeping her cool, "then I suggest you give those figures to him directly, since he'll need to review them anyway."

"No, that wouldn't work," he countered sharply. "If you come with me it'll only take a few minutes. We'd be in and out of my place in, say, half an hour at the most."

Susannah's immediate reaction to situations such as this was a healthy dose of outrage, but she managed to control her temper. "If your apartment is so convenient, then I'll wait here while you go back for those sheets." As she spoke, a couple walked past the tiny table where she was seated with Andrew Adams. Susannah didn't pay much attention to the man, who wore a gray flannel suit, but the blonde with him was striking. Susannah's eyes followed the woman and envied the graceful way she moved.

"It would be easier if you came with me, don't you think?"

"No," she answered bluntly, and lowered her gaze to her glass of white wine. It was then that she felt an odd sensation prickle down her spine. Someone was staring at her; she could feel it as surely as if she were being physically touched. Looking around, Susannah was astonished to discover Nate sitting two tables away. The striking blonde was seated next to him and obviously enjoying his company. She laughed softly and the sound was like a melody, light and breezy.

Susannah's breath caught in her chest, trapped there until the pain reminded her it was time to breathe again. When she did, she reached for her wineglass and succeeded in spilling some of the contents.

Nate's gaze centered on her and then moved to her companion. his mouth thinned and his eyes, which had been so warm and tender a day earlier, now looked as if they could cut through solid rock.

Susannah wasn't exactly thrilled herself. Nate was dating a beauty queen while she was stuck with Donald Duck.

CHAPTER FOUR

SUSANNAH VENTED HER ANGER by pacing the living room carpet. Men! Who needed them?

Not her. Definitely not her! Nate Townsend could take his rainy-day kisses and stuff them in his baseball cap for all she cared. Only he hadn't been wearing that for Miss Universe. Oh no, with the other woman, he was dressed like someone out of *Gentleman's Quarterly*. Susannah, on the other hand, rated worn football jerseys or faded T-shirts.

Susannah hadn't been home more than five minutes when her doorbell chimed. She whirled around and glared at the door as if it were to blame for the intrusion. Checking the peephole, she discovered her caller was Nate. She pulled back, wondering what she should do. He was the last person she wanted to see. He'd made a fool of her... Well, that wasn't entirely true. He'd only made her *feel* like a fool.

"Susannah," he said, knocking impatiently a second time. "I know you're in there."

"Go away."

Her shout was followed by a short pause. "Fine. Have it your way."

Changing her mind, she twisted the lock and yanked open the door. She glared at him with all the fury she could muster—which at the moment was considerable.

Nate glared right back. "Who was that guy?" he asked with an infuriating calm.

She was tempted to inform Nate that it wasn't any of his business. But she decided that would be churlish.

"Andrew Adams," she answered and quickly followed with a demand of her own. "Who was that woman?"

"Sylvia Potter."

For the longest moment, neither spoke.

"That was all I wanted to know," Nate finally said.

"Me, too," she returned stiffly.

Nate retreated two steps, and like precision clockwork Susannah shut the door. "Sylvia Potter," she echoed in a low-pitched voice filled with disdain. "Well, Sylvia Potter, you're welcome to him."

It took another fifteen minutes for the outrage to work its way through her system, but once she'd watched a portion of the evening news and read her mail, she was reasonably calm.

When Susannah really thought about it, what did she have to be so furious about? Nate Townsend didn't mean anything to her. How could he? Until a week ago, she hadn't even known his name.

Okay, so he'd kissed her a couple of times, and sure, there had been electricity, but that was all. Electricity did not constitute a lifetime commitment. If Nate Townsend chose to date every voluptuous blonde between Seattle and New York it shouldn't matter to her.

But it did. And that fact infuriated Susannah more than anything. She didn't want to care about Nate. Her career goals were set. She had drive, determination and a positive mental attitude. But she didn't have Nate.

Jutting out her lower lip, she expelled her breath forcefully, ruffling the dark wisps of hair against her forehead. Maybe it was her hair color—perhaps Nate preferred blondes. He obviously did, otherwise he wouldn't be trying to impress Miss Universe.

Refusing to entertain any more thoughts of her neighbor, Susannah decided to fix herself dinner. An inspection of the freezer revealed a pitifully old chicken patty. Removing it from the cardboard box, Susannah took one look at it and promptly tossed it into the garbage.

Out of the corner of her eye she caught a movement on her balcony. She turned and noted a sleek Siamese cat walking casually along the railing as if he were strolling across a city park.

Although she remained outwardly calm, Susannah's heart lunged to her throat. Her condo was eight floors up. One wrong move and that cat would be history. Carefully walking to her sliding glass door, Susannah eased it open and softly called, "Here, kitty, kitty, kitty."

The cat accepted her invitation and jumped down from the railing. With his tail pointing toward the sky, he walked directly into her apartment and headed straight for the garbage pail, where he stopped.

"I bet you're hungry, aren't you?" she asked softly. She retrieved the chicken patty and stuck it in her microwave. While she stood waiting for it to cook, the cat, with his striking blue eyes and dark brown markings, wove his way in and around her legs, purring madly.

She'd just finished cutting the patty into bite-size pieces and putting it on a plate when her doorbell rang. Licking her fingers clean, she moved into the living room.

"Do you have my cat?" Nate demanded when she opened the door. He'd changed from his suit into jeans and a bright blue T-shirt.

"I don't know," she fibbed. "Describe it."

"Susannah, this isn't time for silly games. Chocolate Chip is a valuable animal."

"Chocolate Chip," she repeated with a soft snicker, crossing her arms and leaning against the doorjamb. "Obviously you didn't read the fine print in the tenant's agreement, because it specifically states in section 12, paragraph 13, that no pets are allowed." Actually she didn't have a clue what section or what paragraph that clause was in, but she wanted him to think she did. "If you don't tattle on me then I won't tattle on you."

"I don't have any pets."

"No, you had a baby."

"But for only three days," she countered. Talk about nit-picking people! He was flagrantly disregarding the rules and had the nerve to throw a minor infraction in her face.

"The cat belongs to my sister. He'll be with me for less than a week. Now, is Chocolate Chip here, or do I go into cardiac arrest?"

"He's here."

Nate visibly relaxed. "Thank God. My sister dotes on that silly feline. She flew up from San Francisco and left him with me before she left for Hawaii." As if he'd heard his name mentioned, Chocolate Chip casually strolled across the carpet and paused at Nate's feet.

Nate bent down to retrieve his sister's cat, scolding him with a harsh look.

"I suggest you keep your balcony door closed," she told him, striving for a flippant air.

"Thanks, I will." Chocolate Chip was tucked under his arm as Nate's gaze casually caught Susannah's. "You may be interested to know that Sylvia Potter's my sister." He turned and walked out her door.

"'Sylvia Potter's my sister,'" Susannah mimicked. It wasn't until she'd closed and locked her door that she realized the import of what he'd said. "His sister," she repeated. "Did he really say that?"

Susannah was at his door before she paused to judge the wisdom of her actions. When Nate answered her furious knock, she stared up at him, her eyes round and confused. "What was that you just said?"

"I said Sylvia Potter's my sister."

"I was afraid of that." Her thoughts were stumbling over one another like marbles tossed out of a bag. She'd imagined . . . she'd assumed. . . .

"Who's Andrew Adams?"

"My brother?" she offered, wondering if he'd believe her.

Nate shook his head. "Try again."

"An associate from H&J Lima," she said, then hurried to explain. "When I canceled my appointment with him Monday morning, he suggested we get together for a drink to discuss business this evening. It sounded innocent enough at the time, but I should have realized it was a mistake. Adams is a known sleazeball."

An appealing smile touched the edges of Nate's mouth. "I wish I'd had a camera with me when you first saw me in that cocktail lounge. I thought your eyes were going to fall out of your face."

"It was your sister—she intimidated me," Susannah admitted. "She's lovely."

"So are you."

The man had obviously been standing too long in the sun, Susannah reasoned. Compared to Sylvia, who was tall, blond and had curves in all the right places, Susannah felt about as pretty as a professional wrestler.

"I'm flattered that you seem to think so." Susannah wasn't comfortable with praise. She was much too levelheaded to let flattery affect her. When men paid her compliments, she smiled and thanked them, but she treated their words like water running off an oily surface.

Except with Nate. Everything was different with him. She seemed to be accumulating a large stack of exceptions because of Nate. As far as Susannah could see, he had no ambitions, and if she'd met him anyplace else other than her building, she probably wouldn't have given him a second thought. Instead she couldn't stop thinking about him. She knew better than to allow her heart to be distracted this way, and yet she couldn't seem to stop herself.

"Do you want to come in?" Nate asked and stepped aside. The bleeping sound drew Susannah's attention across the room to a five-foot-high television screen. She'd apparently interrupted Nate in the middle of an action-packed video game. A video game!

"No," she answered quickly. "I wouldn't want to interrupt you. Besides I was . . . just about to make myself some dinner."

"You cook?"

His astonishment—no, shock—was unflattering, to say the least.

"Of course I do."

"I'm glad to hear it, because I seem to recall that you owe me a meal."

"I—"

"And since we seem to have gotten off on the wrong foot lately, a nice quiet dinner in front of the fireplace sounds like exactly what we need."

Susannah's thoughts were zooming at the speed of light through her befuddled mind. Nate was inviting himself to dinner—one she was supposed to whip up herself! Dear Lord, how could she have so glibly announced that she cooked? Everything she'd ever attempted in the kitchen had been a disaster. Toast was her specialty. Her mind whirled with all the different ways she could serve it. Buttered? With honey? Jam? The list was endless.

"You fix dinner and I'll bring over the wine," Nate said in a low seductive voice. "It's time we sat down together and talked. Deal?"

"I, ah, I've got some papers I need to read over tonight."

"No problem. I'll make it a point to leave early enough for you to finish whatever's necessary."

His eyes held hers for a long moment, and despite everything Susannah knew about Nate, she still wanted time alone with him. She had some papers to review and he had to get back to his video game. A relationship like theirs was not meant to be. However, before she even realized what she was doing, Susannah nodded.

"Good. I'll give you an hour. Is that enough time?"

Once more, like a remote-control robot, she nodded.

Nate smiled and leaned forward to lightly brush his lips over hers. "I'll see you in an hour then."

He put his hand at her lower back and guided her out the door. For a long moment she did nothing more than stand in the hallway, wondering how she was going to get herself out of this one. When she reviewed her options, she realized there was only one choice.

The Western Avenue Deli.

Precisely an hour later, Susannah was ready. A tossed green salad rested in the middle of the table in a crystal bowl, which had been a gift when she graduated from college. Her Aunt Gerty had given it to her. Susannah loved her aunt dearly, but the poor soul had her and Emily confused. Emily would have treasured the fancy bowl. As it happened, this was the first occasion Susannah had even used it and now that she looked at it, she realized that the dish might have been meant for punch. Maybe Nate wouldn't notice. The stroganoff, on the other hand, was simmering in a pan and perfect.

Her doorbell chimed. Susannah drew in a deep breath, then frantically waved her hands over the simmering food to disperse the scent around the condo before she opened her door.

"Hi," Nate said, leaning against the doorjamb. He held a bottle of wine in one hand.

His eyes were so blue, she thought, it was as if she was looking into a crystal-clear lake. When she spoke her voice trembled slightly. "Hi. Dinner's just about ready."

He sniffed the air appreciatively. "Will red wine do?"

"It's perfect," she told him, stepping aside so he could come in.

"Shall I open it now?"

"Please." She led him into the kitchen.

He stopped and cocked an eyebrow. "It looks like you've been busy."

For good measure, Susannah had stacked a few pots and pans in the sink and set out an array of spices on the counter. In addition, she'd laid out a few books. None of them had anything to do with cooking—she didn't own any cookbooks—but they looked impressive.

"I hope you like stroganoff," she said cheerfully. "It's one of my favorites."

Susannah swallowed tightly and nodded. She'd never been much good at deception, but then she'd rarely put her pride on the line the way she was this evening.

While she dished up the stroganoff, Nate expertly opened the wine and poured them each a glass. When he'd finished, they sat across the table from each other.

After one taste of the buttered noodles and the rich sauce, Nate said, "This is delicious."

Susannah kept her gaze lowered. "Thanks. My mother has a recipe that's been handed down for years." It was a half-truth that was stretched about as far it could go without snapping back and hitting her in the face. Yes, her mother did have a favorite family recipe, but it was for Christmas candies.

"The salad is excellent, too. What's in the dressing?"

This was the moment Susannah had dreaded. "Ah..." Her mind faltered before she could remember exactly what usually went into salad dressings. "Oil!" she cried, as if black gold had just been discovered in her living room.

"Vinegar?"

"Yes." She nodded eagerly. "Lots of that."

Planting his elbows on the table, he smiled at her. "Spices?"

"Oh, yes, those, too."

His mouth was quivering when he took a sip of wine.

Subterfuge had never been Susannah's strong point. If Nate hadn't started asking her these difficult questions, she might have been able to pull off the ruse. But he obviously knew, and there wasn't any reason to continue it.

"Nate," she said, after fortifying herself with a sip of wine, "I . . . I didn't exactly cook this meal myself."

"The Western Avenue Deli?"

She nodded, feeling wretched.

"An excellent choice."

"H-how'd you know?" Something inside her demanded further abuse. Anyone else would have dropped the matter right then.

"You mean other than the fact that you've got enough pots and pans in your sink to have fed a small army? By the way, what could you possibly have used the broiler pan for?"

"I . . . was hoping you'd think I'd warmed the noodles on it."

"I see." He was doing an admirable job of not laughing outright, and Susannah supposed she should be grateful for that much.

After taking a bite of the dinner roll, he asked, "Where'd you get all the spices?"

"They were a Christmas gift from Emily one year. She continues to hold out hope that a miracle will happen and I'll suddenly discover I've missed my calling in life and decide to chain myself to the stove."

Nate grinned as if he found the picture an amusing one. "For future reference, I can't see how you'd need poultry seasoning or curry powder for stroganoff."

"Oh." She should have quit when she was ahead. "So . . . you knew right from the first?"

Nate nodded. "I'm afraid so, but I'm flattered by all the trouble you went to."

"I suppose it won't do any more harm to admit that I'm a total loss in the kitchen. I'd rather analyze a profit-and-loss statement any day than attempt to bake a batch of cookies."

Nate reached for a second dinner roll. "If you ever do, my favorite are chocolate chip."

"I'll remember that." An outlet for Rainy Day Cookies had recently opened up on the waterfront and they were the best money could buy.

Nate helped her clear the table once they'd finished. While she rinsed the plates and put them in the dishwasher, Nate built a fire. He was seated on the floor in front of the fireplace waiting for her when she entered the room.

"More wine?" he asked, holding up the bottle.

"Please." Inching her straight skirt slightly higher, Susannah carefully lowered herself to the carpet next to him. Nate grinned and reached for the light, turning it to the lowest setting. Shadows from the fire flickered across the opposite wall. The atmosphere was warm and cozy.

"All right," he said softly, close to her ear. "Ask away."

Susannah blinked, not sure what he meant.

"You've been dying of curiosity about me from the moment we met. I'm simply giving you the opportunity to ask me anything you want."

Susannah gulped her wine. If he could read her so easily, then she had no place in the business world. Yes, she was full of questions about him, and had been trying to find a way to bring some of them subtly into the conversation.

"First, however," he said, "let me do this."

Before she knew what was happening, Nate had pressed her down onto the carpet and was kissing her. Kissing her deeply, drugging her senses with a mastery that was just short of arrogant. He'd caught her unprepared, and before she could raise any defenses, she was captured in a dizzying wave of sensation.

When he lifted his head, Susannah stared up at him, breathless and amazed at her own ready response. Before she could react, Nate reached behind her. He unpinned her hair, then ran his fingers through it.

"I've been wanting to do that all night," he murmured.

Still she couldn't speak. He'd kissed and held her but these actions didn't seem to affect his powers of speech, while she felt completely flustered and perplexed.

"Yes, well," she managed to mutter, righting herself. "I ... forget what we were talking about."

Nate moved behind her and pulled her against his chest, wrapping his arms around her and nibbling on the side of her neck as if she were a delectable dessert. He paused long enough to answer her question. "I believe you were about to ask me something."

"Yes ... you're right, I was ... Nate, do you work?"

"No."

Delicious shivers were racing up and down her spine. His teeth found her earlobe and he sucked gently on that, causing her insides to quake in seismic proportions.

"Why not?" she asked, her voice trembling.

"I quit."

"But why?"

"I was working too hard. I wasn't enjoying myself anymore."

"Oh."

His mouth had progressed down the gentle slope of her neck to her shoulder, and she closed her eyes to the warring emotions churning inside her. Part of her longed to surrender to the thrill of his touch, yet she hungered to know all she could about this unconventional man.

Nate altered his position so he was in front of her once more. He kissed her gently and then his mouth began exploring her face with soft kisses that fell like gentle raindrops over her eyes, nose, cheeks and lips.

"Anything else you want to know?" he asked, pausing.

Unable to do more than shake her head, Susannah sighed and reluctantly unwound her arms from around his neck.

"Do you want more wine?" he asked.

"No...thank you." It demanded all the fortitude she possessed not to ask him to keep kissing her.

"Okay," he said, making himself comfortable. He leaned forward and wrapped his arms around his knees. "My turn."

"Your turn?"

"Yes," he said with a lazy grin that did wicked things to her equilibrium. "I have a few questions for you."

Susannah found it difficult to center her attention on anything other than the fact that Nate was sitting not more than a few inches away from her and could lean over and kiss her again at any moment.

"You don't object?"

"No," she said, gesturing with her hand.

"Okay, tell me more about yourself."

Susannah paused. For the life of her, she couldn't think of a single thing that would impress him. She'd worked hard, climbing the corporate ladder, inching her way toward her long-range goals.

"I'm up for promotion," she began. "I started working for H&J Lima five years ago. I chose this company, although the pay was less than what I'd been offered by two others.''

"Why?''

"There's opportunity with them. I looked at the chain of command and saw room for steady advancement. Being a woman is both an asset and a detriment, if you know what I mean. I had to work hard to prove myself, but I was also aware of being the token woman on the staff.''

"You mean you were hired *because* you were female?''

"Exactly. But I swallowed my pride and set about proving that I could handle anything asked of me, and I have.''

Nate looked proud of her.

"Five years ago, I decided I wanted to be the vice president in charge of marketing,'' she said, her voice gaining strength and conviction in pace with her enthusiasm. "It was a significant goal, because I'd be the first woman to hold a position that high within the company.''

"And?''

"And I'll find out in the next few weeks if I'm going to get it. I'll derive a good deal of satisfaction from recognizing that I earned it. I won't be their token female in upper management any longer.''

"What's the competition like?''

Susannah slowly expelled her breath. "Stiff. Damn stiff. There are two men in the running, and both have been with the company as long as me, and in one case longer. Both are older, bright and dedicated.''

"You're bright and dedicated, too.''

"That may not be enough," she murmured. Now that her dream was within reach, she yearned for it even more. She could feel Nate's eyes studying her.

"This promotion means a lot to you, doesn't it?"

"Yes. It's everything. From the moment I was hired, I've striven toward this very thing. But it's happening much faster than I dared hope."

Nate was silent for a moment when she'd finished. He put another log on the fire, and although she hadn't asked for it, he replenished her wine.

"Have you ever stopped to think what would happen if you achieved your dreams and then discovered you weren't happy?"

"How could I not be happy?" she asked. She honestly didn't understand. For years she'd striven toward obtaining this vice presidency. Of course she was going to be happy. She'd be thrilled, elated, jubilant.

Nate's gaze narrowed. "Aren't you worried about there being a void in your life?"

Oh, no, he was beginning to sound like Emily. "No," she said flatly. "How could there be? Now before you start, I know what you're going to say, so please don't. Save your breath. Emily has argued with me about this very subject from the time I graduated from college."

Nate looked genuinely puzzled. "Argued with you about what?"

"Getting married and having a family. The roles of wife and mother just aren't for me. They never have been and they never will be."

"I see."

Susannah was equally convinced he didn't. "If I were a man, would everyone be pushing me to marry?"

Nate chuckled and his eyes rested on her for a tantalizing moment. "Trust me, Susannah, no one is going to mistake you for a man."

She grinned and lowered her gaze. "It's the nose, isn't it?"

"The nose?"

"Yes." She twisted sideways and held her head at a lofty angle in order for him to view her classic profile. "I think it's my best feature." The wine had obviously gone to her head. But that was all right because she felt warm and cozy and Nate was sitting beside her. Rarely had she been more content.

"Actually I wasn't thinking about your nose at all. I was remembering that first night with Michelle."

"You mean when we both fell asleep in the living room?"

Nate nodded and reached for her shoulder, his eyes trapping hers. "It was the only time in my life I can remember having one woman in my arms and wanting another."

CHAPTER FIVE

"I'VE DECIDED not to see him again," Susannah announced.

"I beg your pardon?" Ms Brooks stopped in her tracks and looked at her boss.

Unnerved, Susannah made busywork at her desk. "I'm sorry, I didn't realize I'd spoken aloud."

Her secretary delivered the coffee to her desk and hesitated. "How late did you end up staying last night?"

"Not long," Susannah lied. It had, in fact, been almost ten when she left the building.

"And the night before?" Ms Brooks pressed.

"Not so late," Susannah fibbed again.

Eleanor Brooks quietly left the room, but not before she gave Susannah a stern look, which said she didn't believe her for one moment.

As soon as the door closed, Susannah pressed the tips of her fingers to her forehead and exhaled a slow steady breath. Dear heaven, Nate Townsend had her so twisted up inside she was talking to the walls.

Nate hadn't left her condo until almost eleven the night he'd come for dinner, and by that time he'd kissed her nearly senseless. Three days had passed and Susannah could still taste and feel his mouth on hers. The scent of his after-shave lingered in her living room to the

point that she looked for him every time she walked into
the room.

The man didn't even hold down a job. Oh, he'd had
one, but he'd quit and it was obvious, to her at least,
that he wasn't in any hurry to get another. He'd held her
and kissed her and patiently listened to her dreams. But
he hadn't shared any of his own. He had no ambitions,
and no urge to better himself.

And Susannah was falling head over heels for him.

Through the years, she had assumed she was im-
mune to falling in love. She was too sensible for that,
too practical, too career oriented. Not once did she
suspect she would fall so hard for someone like Nate.
Nate, with his no-need-to-rush attitude and tomorrow-
will-take-care-of-itself life-style.

Realizing what was happening to her, Susannah had
done the only thing she could—gone into hiding. For
three days she'd managed to avoid Nate. He'd left a
couple of messages on her answering machine, which
she'd ignored. If he confronted her, she had a perfect
excuse. She was working. And it was true: she spent
much of her time holed up in the office. She left home
early in the morning and arrived home late at night. The
extra hours she was putting in served two distinct purposes: they showed her employer that she was dedicated, and kept her from having to deal with Nate.

Her intercom buzzed, effectively pulling Susannah
from her thoughts. She reached over and pressed down
the button. "Yes?"

"Mr. Townsend is on the phone."

Susannah squeezed her eyes closed and her throat
muscles tightened. "Take a message," she said, her
voice little more than a husky whisper.

"He insists on speaking to you."

"Tell him I'm in a meeting and . . . unavailable."

That wasn't like Susannah to lie, and her secretary knew it.

Ms Brooks hesitated and then asked, "Is this the man you plan never to see again?"

The abruptness of her secretary's questions caught Susannah off guard. "Yes . . ."

"I thought as much. I'll tell him you're not available."

"Thank you." Susannah's hand was trembling by the time she released the intercom button. She hadn't dreamed Nate would call her at the office.

By eleven, a feeling of normalcy had returned. Susannah was gathering together her notes for an executive meeting with the finance committee when her secretary entered her office. "Franklin phoned and canceled his afternoon appointment."

Susannah paused. "Did he want to reschedule?"

"Friday at ten."

She nodded. "That'll be fine." It was on the tip of her tongue to ask her secretary how Nate had responded earlier when told she was unavailable, but she resisted the temptation.

"Mr. Townsend left a message."

Her secretary knew her too well, it seemed, and could read her thoughts. "Leave it on my desk."

"You might want to read it," the older woman urged, looking flustered.

"I will. Later."

Halfway through the meeting, Susannah wished she'd followed her assistant's advice. Impatience filled her. She wanted this finance meeting over so she could hurry back to her desk and read the message from Nate. Figures flew over head—important ones with bearing on the outcome of the marketing strategy she and her department had planned. Yet, again and again, Susannah found her thoughts drifting to Nate.

That wasn't like her. When the meeting finally ended, she was furious with herself. She walked briskly back to her office, her low heels making staccato taps against the polished hardwood floor.

"Ms Brooks," she said, as she hurried into the outer office. "Could you—"

Susannah stopped dead in her tracks. The last person she'd expected to see was Nate. He was sitting on the corner of her secretary's desk, wearing a Mariners T-shirt, faded jeans and a baseball cap. He tossed a hardball in the air and deftly caught it in his mitt.

Eleanor Brooks looked both unsettled and inordinately pleased. No doubt Nate had used some of his considerable male charm on the gray-haired grandmother.

"It's about time," Nate said, grinning devilishly. He leaped off the corner of the desk. "I was afraid we were going to be late for the game."

"Game?" Susannah repeated. "What game?"

Nate held out his right hand to show her his baseball mitt and ball—just in case she hadn't noticed them earlier. "The Mariners are playing, and I've got two of the best seats in the place reserved for you and me."

Susannah's heart sank to the pit of her stomach. It was just like Nate to assume she could take off in the middle of the day on some lark. He obviously had no understanding of what being a responsible employee meant. It was bad enough that he'd dominated her thoughts through an important meeting, but suggesting they escape for an afternoon was too much.

"You don't honestly expect me to leave, do you?"

"Yes."

"I can't. I won't."

"Why not?"

"I'm working," she said, deciding that was enough explanation.

"You've been at the office late every night this week. You need a break. Come on, Susannah, let your hair down long enough to have a good time. It isn't going to hurt. I promise."

He was so casual about the whole thing, as if obligation and duty were of little significance. It proved more than anything that he didn't grasp the concept of hard work being its own reward.

"It will hurt," she argued.

"Okay," he said forcefully. "What's so important this afternoon?" To answer his own question, he walked around her secretary's desk. Then he leaned forward and flipped open the pages of her appointment schedule.

"Mr. Franklin canceled his three o'clock appointment," Ms Brooks reminded her primly. "And you skipped lunch because of the finance meeting."

Susannah glared at the older woman, wondering what exactly Nate had said or done that had turned her loyal secretary into a traitor on such short acquaintance.

"I have other more important things to do," Susannah told them both stiffly.

"Not according to your appointment schedule," Nate returned confidently. "As far as I can see you haven't got an excuse in the world not to attend that baseball game with me."

Susannah wasn't going to stand there and argue with him. Instead she marched into her office with a precision step General George Patton would have admired and dutifully sat down at her desk.

To her chagrin both Nate and Ms Brooks followed her inside. It was all Susannah could do not to bury her face in her hands and demand they both leave.

"Susannah," Nate coaxed gently, "you need a break. Tomorrow you'll come back rejuvenated and refreshed. If you spend as many hours at the office as you have lately, you'll begin to lose some of your perspective. An afternoon away will do you a world of good."

Her secretary looked as if she were about to comment, but Susannah stopped her with a scalding look. Before she could say anything to Nate, someone else entered her office.

"Susannah, I was just looking over these figures and I—" John Hammer stopped midsentence when he noticed the two other people in her office.

If there had been an open window handy, Susannah would have gladly hurled herself through it. The company director smiled benignly, however, looking slightly embarrassed at having interrupted her. Now, it seemed, he was awaiting an introduction.

"John, this is Nate Townsend . . . my neighbor."

Ever the gentleman, John stepped forward and extended his hand. If he thought it a bit odd to find a man in Susannah's office dressed in jeans and a jersey, he didn't show it.

"Nate Townsend," he repeated, pumping his hand. "It's a pleasure, a real pleasure."

"Thank you," Nate returned. "I'm here to pick up Susannah. We're going to a Mariners game this afternoon."

John removed the glasses from the end of his nose, and looked thoughtful. "An excellent idea."

"No, I really don't think I'll go. I mean..." She stopped when it became obvious that no one was paying any attention to her protests.

"Nate's absolutely right," John said, setting the file on her desk. "You've been putting in a lot of extra hours lately. Take the afternoon off. Enjoy yourself."

"But—"

"Susannah, are you actually going to argue with your boss?" Nate prompted.

Her jaw sagged. "I...guess not."

"Good. Good." John looked as pleased as if he'd made the suggestion himself. He was smiling at Nate and nodding as if the two were longtime friends.

Her expression more than a little smug, Eleanor Brooks returned to her own office.

Nate glanced at his watch. "We'd better leave now or we'll miss the opening pitch."

With heavy reluctance, Susannah reached for her purse. She'd done everything within her power to avoid Nate, yet through no fault of her own, she was going to spend the afternoon in his company. They didn't get a chance to speak until they reached the elevator, but as soon as the door glided shut, Susannah tried once more. "I can't go to a baseball game dressed like this."

"You look fine to me."

"But I've got a business suit on."

"Hey, don't sweat the small stuff." His hand reached for hers and when the elevator door opened on the bottom floor, he led her out of the building. Once outside, he quickened his pace as he headed down Fourth Avenue toward the Kingdome.

"I want you to know I don't appreciate this one bit," she said, forced to half run to keep pace with his long-legged stride.

"If you're going to complain, wait until we're inside and settled. As I recall, you get testy on an empty stomach." His smile was enough to cause a nuclear meltdown, but she was determined not to let it influence her. Nate had a lot of nerve to come bursting into her office, and as soon as she could catch her breath, she'd tell him so.

"Don't worry, I'm going to feed you," he promised, when they were forced to wait at a red light.

His assurance did little to smooth her ruffled feathers. Lord only knew what John Hammer thought—although she had to admit that her employer's reaction had baffled her. John was as hardworking and dedicated as Susannah herself. It wasn't like him to fall in with Nate's offbeat idea of attending a ball game in the middle of the afternoon. In fact, it almost seemed as if John knew Nate, or had heard of him. Hardly ever had she seen her employer show such enthusiasm when introduced to anyone.

The man at the Kingdome gate took their tickets and Nate directed her to a pair of seats right behind home plate. Never having attended a professional baseball game before, Susannah didn't realize how good these seats actually were.

She'd no sooner sat down in her place when Nate leaped to his feet and raised his right hand. Susannah slouched as low as she could in the unyielding seat. The next thing she knew, a bag of peanuts whizzed past her ear.

"Hey!" she cried, and jerked around.

"Don't panic," Nate said, and chuckled. "I'm just playing catch with the vendor." No sooner had the words parted from his mouth when he expertly caught a second bag.

"Here." Nate handed her both bags. "The hot dog guy will be by in a minute."

Susannah had no intention of sitting still while food was being tossed about. "I'm getting out of here. If you want to play ball, go on the field."

Once more Nate laughed, the sound husky and rich. "If you're going to balk at every little thing, I know a good way to settle you down."

"Do you think I'm a complete idiot? First you drag me away from my office, then you insist on throwing food around like some schoolboy. I can't even begin to guess what's going to happen next, and another thing—"

She didn't get any further, although her outrage was mounting with every breath she drew. Before she could guess his intention, Nate planted his hands on her shoulders, hauled her against him and gave her one of his dynamite-packed kisses.

Completely unnerved, she numbly lowered herself back into her seat and closed her eyes, her pulse roaring in her ears.

The next thing she knew, Nate was pressing a fat hot dog into her lifeless hands. "I had them put everything on it," he explained.

A glance at the overstuffed bun informed her that "everything" included pickles, mustard, ketchup, onions and sauerkraut and one or two more items she wasn't sure she could identify.

"Now eat it before I'm forced to kiss you again."

His warning was all the incentive she needed. Several minutes had passed since he'd last kissed her and she was still so bemused she could hardly think. On cue, she lifted the hot dog to her mouth, prepared for the worst. But to her surprise, it didn't taste half bad. In fact, it was downright palatable. When she'd polished it off, she reached for the peanuts, which were still warm from the roaster. Warm and salty, and excellent.

Another vendor strolled past and Nate bought them each a cold drink.

The first inning was over by the time Susannah finished eating. Nate reached for her hand. "Feel better?" His eyes were friendly enough to warm water.

One look certainly had full effect on Susannah. Every time her eyes met his she felt as if she were caught in a whirlpool and about to be sucked under. She'd tried to resist the pull, but it had been impossible.

"Susannah?" he prompted.

It was all she could do to nod. After a moment she said, "I still feel a little foolish though...."

"Why?"

"Come on, Nate. I'm the only person here in a business suit, for heaven's sake."

"I can fix that."

"Oh?" Susannah sincerely had her doubts. What did he plan to do? Undress her?

He gave her another one of his famous knowing smiles and casually excused himself. Puzzled, Susannah watched as he made his way toward the concession stand. Then minutes later he was back with a Mariner jersey in one hand, a baseball cap in the other.

Removing her suit jacket, Susannah slipped the jersey over her head. When she was finished, Nate set the baseball cap on her head, adjusting it so the bill dipped low over her forehead.

"There," he said, satisfied. "You look like one of the home team now."

"Thanks." She smoothed the T-shirt over her straight skirt and wondered at the sight she made. Funny how it didn't seem to matter. She was having a good time with Nate, and it felt wonderful to laugh and enjoy life.

"You're welcome."

They both settled back in their seats to give their full attention to the game. The Seattle Mariners were down by one run at the bottom of the fifth inning.

Susannah didn't know all that much about baseball, but the crowd was a good size and seemed to be lending its support to the home team. She loved the organ music and the atmosphere, which crackled with excitement, as if everyone was waiting for something splendid to happen.

"You've been avoiding me," Nate said halfway through the sixth inning. "I want to know why."

She couldn't very well tell him the truth, but lying seemed equally unattractive. Pretending to focus her attention on the field, Susannah shrugged, hoping he'd accept that as explanation enough.

"Susannah?"

She should have known he would force the issue. "Because I don't like what happens when you kiss me," she blurted out.

"What happens?" he echoed. "The first time we kissed, you nearly dealt my ego a fatal blow. As I recall, you claimed it was a pleasant experience. I believe you described it as 'nice,' and said that was about it."

Susannah kicked at the litter on the cement floor with the toes of her pumps, her gaze downcast. "Yes, I do remember saying something along those lines."

"You lied?"

He didn't need to drill her to prove his point. "All right," she admitted, "I lied. But you knew that all along. You must have, otherwise..."

"Otherwise what?"

"You wouldn't be kissing me every time you want to coerce me into doing something I don't want to do."

Crow's-feet fanned out at the edges of his eyes as he grinned, making him look both naughty and angelic at once.

"You knew all along, so don't give me that injured-ego routine!"

"It feels good for you to admit it. There's electricity between us, Susannah, and it's about time you recognized that. I did, from the very first."

"Sure. But there's a big difference between standing next to an electrical outlet and fooling around with a high-voltage wire. I prefer to play it safe."

"Not me." He ran a knuckle down the side of her face. Circling her chin, his finger rested on her lips, which parted as if by demand. "No," he said in a hushed voice, studying her. "I always did prefer to live dangerously."

"I've noticed." Nerve endings tingled at his touch, and Susannah held her breath until he removed his hand. Only then did she breathe normally once again.

The cheering crowd alerted her to the fact that something important had taken place in the game. Glad to have her attention diverted from Nate, she watched as a Mariner rounded the bases for a home run. Pleased, she clapped politely, although her enthusiasm was far more restrained than that of the other spectators around her.

That changed, however, at the bottom of the ninth inning. The bases were loaded and Susannah sat on the edge of her seat as the designated hitter approached home plate.

The spectators around her were chanting, "Grand slam, grand slam!" and Susannah's voice soon joined in. The pitcher tossed a fast ball, and unable to watch, she squeezed her eyes shut. But the sound of the wood hitting the ball was immediately recognizable. Susannah opened her eyes and leaped to her feet as the ball flew into left field and over the wall. The crowd went wild, and after doing an impulsive jig, Susannah threw her arms around Nate's neck and hugged him.

Nate appeared equally excited, and when Susannah had her feet back on the ground once more, he raised his fingers to his mouth and let loose a piercing whistle.

She was laughing and cheering and even went so far as to cup her hands along the sides of her mouth and boisterously yell her approval. It was then that she noticed Nate watching her. His eyes were wide with feigned shock, as if he couldn't believe the refined and cultured Susannah Simmons would dare to lower herself to such enthusiastic approval.

His censure instantly cooled her reactions, and she returned to her seat and demurely folded her hands and crossed her ankles, embarrassed now by her uninhibited response to something as mindless as a baseball game. When she dared to glance in Nate's direction, she discovered him watching her intently.

"Nate," she whispered, disconcerted by his undivided attention. The game was over and everyone around them had started to leave their seats. Susannah could feel the color in her cheeks. "Why are you looking at me like that?"

"You amaze me."

More likely, she'd disgraced herself in his eyes by her wild display. She was mortified.

"You're going to be all right, Susannah Simmons," he announced cryptically. "We both are."

"SUSANNAH, I'M SURPRISED to find you home on a Saturday," Emily said as she stepped inside her sister's apartment. "Michelle and I are going to the Pike Place Market this morning and decided to drop by and see you first. You don't mind, do you?"

"No. Of course not. Come in." Susannah brushed the hair from her face and wiped the sleep from her eyes. "What time is it anyway?"

"Eight-thirty."

"That late, huh?"

Emily chuckled. "I forgot. You like to sleep in on the weekends, don't you?"

"Don't worry about it," she said on the tail end of a yawn. "I'll put on a pot of coffee and be myself in no time."

Emily and Michelle followed her into the kitchen. Once the coffee was brewing, Susannah took the chair across from her sister. Michelle gleefully waved her arms, and despite the early hour, Susannah found herself smiling at her niece's enthusiasm toward life. She held out her arms to the baby and was pleasantly surprised when Michelle happily came into them.

"I think she remembers you," Emily said, sounding amazed.

"Of course she does," Susannah said as she nuzzled her niece's neck. "We had some great times, didn't we, kiddo? Especially when it came to feeding you the plums."

Emily chuckled. "I don't know that I'll ever be able to thank you enough for keeping Michelle that weekend. That time away was just what Robert and I needed."

"Don't mention it." Susannah dismissed the appreciation with a weak gesture of her hand. She was the one who'd profited from that zany weekend. It might have been several weeks before she'd met Nate if it hadn't been for Michelle.

Emily sighed. "I've been trying for the past week to get hold of you, but you're never home."

"Why didn't you leave a message on the machine?"

Emily shook her head and her long braid swung with the action. "You know I hate those things. I get all tongue-tied and I can't seem to talk. You might phone me sometime, you know."

Over the past couple of weeks, Susannah had considered it, but she'd been avoiding her sister because she knew that the minute she called, Emily was going to ply her with questions about Nate.

"Have you been working late every night?" Emily asked.

Susannah lowered her gaze. "Not exactly."

"Then you must have been out with Nate Townsend." Emily didn't give her time to respond, but immediately started jabbering away like a blue jay. "I don't mind telling you, Susannah, both Robert and I were impressed with your new neighbor. He was wonderful with Michelle, and from the way he was looking at you, I think he's interested. Now, please, don't tell me to keep my nose out of this. You're twenty-eight, for heaven's sake, and that biological clock is ticking away every single day. If you're ever going to settle down and get serious about a man, the time is now. And personally, I don't think you'll find anyone better than Nate. Why he's..."

She paused to breathe, giving Susannah the chance she'd been waiting for. "Coffee?"

Emily blinked, then nodded. "You didn't listen to a word I said, did you?"

"I listened."

"But you didn't *hear* a single word."

"Sure I did," Susannah countered. "I'd be a fool not to put a ring through Nate Townsend's nose. You want me to marry him before I lose my very last chance at motherhood."

"Exactly," Emily said, looking pleased that she'd conveyed her message so effectively.

Michelle squirmed and Susannah set her on the floor to crawl around and explore.

"Well?" Emily pressed. "What do you think?"

"About marrying Nate? It would never work," she said calmly, as though they were discussing something as mundane as stock options, "for more reasons than you realize. But to satisfy your curiosity I'll list a few. First and foremost I've got a career and he doesn't, and furthermore—"

"Nate's unemployed?" her sister gasped. "But how can he not work? I mean this is an expensive complex. Didn't you tell me the condominium next to yours was nearly twice as large? How can he afford to live there if he doesn't have a job?"

"I have no idea."

Susannah forgot about Nate for the moment as her eyes followed Michelle. It was something of a surprise to realize how much she'd missed her. She stood and brought down two cups from the cupboard.

"That's not decaffeinated, is it?" Emily asked.

"No."

"Then don't bother pouring me a cup. I gave up caffeine years ago."

"Right." Susannah should have remembered. Michelle crawled across the kitchen floor to her and, using Susannah's nightgown for leverage, pulled herself into a standing position. She smiled merrily at her achievement.

"Listen," Susannah said impulsively, leaning over to pick up her niece. "Why don't you leave Michelle with me? We'll take this morning to become reacquainted and you do your shopping without having to worry about her."

A short shocked silence followed. "Susannah?" Emily said, after a moment. "Did I hear you correctly? I thought I just heard you volunteer to baby-sit Michelle."

CHAPTER SIX

THE MORNING WAS BRIGHT and sunny, and unable to resist, Susannah opened the sliding glass door and let the salty breeze off Elliott Bay blow into her apartment. Sitting on the kitchen floor with a saucepan and a wooden spoon, Michelle lightheartedly proceeded to demonstrate her musical talents by pounding out a loud enthusiastic beat.

When the phone rang, Susannah knew it was Nate.

"Good morning," she said, brushing the hair away from her face. She hadn't pinned it up when she'd dressed, knowing Nate preferred it down, and she didn't try to fool herself with excuses for leaving it that way.

"Morning," he breathed into the phone. "Do you have a drummer visiting?"

"No, a special friend. I think she'd like to say hello. Hold on a minute." Susannah put down the telephone receiver and lifted Michelle from the floor. Holding the baby on her hip, she pressed the telephone receiver to the side of Michelle's face. As if on cue, the child let loose an excited flow of gibberish.

"I think she said good-morning," Susannah explained.

"Michelle?"

"How many other babies would pay me a visit?"

"How many Simmons girls are there?"

"Only Emily and me," she answered with a soft laugh, "but trust me, the two of us were enough for any one set of parents to handle."

Nate's responding chuckle was warm and seductive. "Are you in the mood for more company?"

"Sure. If you bring the Danish, I'll provide the coffee."

"You've got yourself a deal."

It wasn't until several minutes had passed that Susannah realized how little resistance she was putting up lately when it came to Nate. Since the baseball game, she'd given up trying to avoid him; she simply hadn't the heart for it, although deep down, she knew anything beyond friendship was impossible. Yet despite her misgivings, after that one afternoon with him she'd come away feeling exhilarated and excited. Being with Nate was like recapturing a part of her youth that had somehow escaped her. Seeing him was fun, true, but it wasn't meant to last, and Susannah reminded herself of that fact every time they were together. Nate Townsend was like an unexpected burst of sunshine on an overcast day, but soon the rain would come, the way it always did. Susannah wasn't going to be fooled into believing there could ever be anything permanent between them.

When Nate arrived, the reunion was complete. He lifted Michelle high into the air and Susannah smiled at the little girl's squeals of delight.

"Where's Emily?" he wanted to know.

"Shopping. She won't be more than an hour or so."

With Michelle in one arm, Nate moved into the kitchen where Susannah was dishing up the pastries and pouring coffee. "She's grown, hasn't she?" she said.

"Is that another new tooth?" he asked, peering inside the baby's mouth.

"It might be," Susannah replied, taking a look herself.

Nate wrapped his free arm around her shoulder and smiled at her. His eyes, so clear and blue, were enough to rob her of her wits.

"Your hair's down," he murmured, his look caressing her upturned face.

She nodded, not knowing how else to respond, although a dozen plausible excuses raced through her mind. But none of them would have been true.

"For me?"

Once more, she answered him with a slight nod.

"Thank you," he whispered, his face so close to her own that his words were like a gentle kiss.

Hardly realizing what she was doing, Susannah leaned into him, pressing herself against his solid length. When he kissed her, it was all she could do not to melt into his arms.

Michelle thought it was great fun to have two adults so close. She wove her fingers into Susannah's hair and yanked until Susannah was forced to pull away from Nate.

Smiling, Nate disengaged the baby's hand from her aunt's hair and kissed Susannah once more. "Hmm," he said when he lifted his head. "You taste better than any sweet roll ever could."

Unnerved, and suddenly feeling more than a little shy, Susannah busied herself setting the pastries on the table.

"Do you have plans for today?" he asked, taking a chair, Michelle gurgling happily on his lap.

Michelle was content for the moment, but from experience Susannah knew she'd want to be back on the floor soon. "I . . . I was thinking of going into the office for an hour or so."

"I don't think so," Nate returned flatly.

"You don't?" she asked, somewhat surprised.

"I'm taking you out." He paused and surveyed her navy-blue slacks and the winter-white sweater she wore. "I don't suppose you have any jeans."

Susannah nodded. She knew she did, somewhere, but it was years since she'd worn them. As long ago as college, and maybe even her last year of high school. "I don't know if they'll fit, though."

"Go try them on."

"Why? What are you planning? Knowing you, I could end up on top of Mount Rainier looking over a crevasse, and not know how I got there."

"We're going to fly a kite today," he announced casually, as if it was something they'd done several times.

Susannah thought she'd misunderstood him. Nate loved pulling this kind of surprise. First a baseball game in the middle of a workday, and now kites?

"You heard me right, so don't stand there with your eyes as wide as Grand Coulee Dam."

"But . . . kites . . . that's for kids. Frankly, Nate," she said, her voice gaining some conviction, "I don't happen to have one stuffed away in any closet. Besides, isn't that something parents do with their children?"

"No, it's for everyone. Don't look so indignant. Adults have been known to have fun, too. Don't worry about a thing. I built a huge one and it's ready for testing."

"A kite?" she repeated, holding in the desire to laugh outright. She'd been in grade school the last time she'd attempted anything so...so juvenile.

By the time Susannah had rummaged in her closet and found an old pair of jeans, Emily had returned for Michelle. Nate let her sister inside, but the bedroom door was cracked open, and Susannah could hear the conversation. She held her breath, first because her hips were a tiny bit wider than the last time she'd donned her denims, and also because Susannah could never be sure what her sister was going to say. Or do.

It would be just like Emily to start telling Nate how suitable Susannah would be as a wife. That thought was sobering enough to make Susannah stop short.

"Nate," she heard her sister say, "it's so good of you to help with Michelle." Her voice was a full octave higher than usual in her excitement.

"No problem. Susannah will be out in a minute—she's putting on a pair of jeans. We're going to Gas Works Park to fly a kite."

There was a short pause. "Susannah wearing jeans and flying a kite? You mean she's actually going with you?"

"Of course I am. Don't look so shocked," Susannah said, walking into the room. "How did the shopping go?"

Emily couldn't seem to close her mouth. She stared at her sister to the point of embarrassment, then swung her gaze to Nate and back to Susannah again.

Susannah realized she must look different, wearing jeans and with her hair down, but it certainly didn't warrant this openmouthed gawking.

"Emily?" Susannah waved her hand in front of her sister's face in an effort to bring her back to earth.

"Oh . . . the shopping went just fine. I was able to get the fresh herbs I wanted. Basil and thyme and . . . some others." As though in a daze, Emily lifted the home-sewn bag draped over her arm as evidence of her successful trip to the market.

"Good," Susannah said enthusiastically, wanting to smooth over her sister's outrageous reaction. "Michelle wasn't a bit of trouble. If you need me to watch her again, just say so."

Her sister's eyes grew wider. She swallowed and nodded. "Thanks. I'll remember that."

THE SKY WAS AS BLUE as Nate's eyes, Susannah thought, sitting with her knees tucked under her chin on the lush green grass of Gas Works Park. The wind whipped Nate's box kite back and forth as he scrambled from one hill to the next, letting the brisk breeze carry the multicolored crate in several directions. As it was late September, Susannah didn't expect many more glorious Indian summer days like this one.

She closed her eyes and soaked up the sun. Her spirits raced with the kites that abounded in the popular park. She felt like tossing back her head and laughing triumphantly, for no other reason than that it felt good to be alive.

"I'm beat," Nate said, dropping on the grass beside her. He lay on his back, his arms and legs spread-eagle.

"Where's the kite?"

"I gave it to one of the kids who didn't have one."

Susannah smiled. That sounded exactly like something Nate would do. He'd spent hours designing and constructing the box kite, and yet he impulsively gave it away without a second thought.

"Actually I begged the kid to take it, before I keeled over from exhaustion," he amended. "Don't let anyone tell you otherwise. Flying a kite is hard work."

Work was a subject Susannah stringently avoided discussing with Nate. From the first he'd been completely open with her. Open and honest. She was confident that if she quizzed him about his profession or lack of one, he'd answer her truthfully.

Basically, Susannah supposed, what she didn't know about him couldn't upset her. Nate apparently had a good deal of money. He certainly didn't seem troubled by financial difficulties. But it was his attitude that worried her. He seemed to see life as just one grand adventure. He leaped from one interest to another without apparent rhyme or reason. Nothing seemed more important or vital than the moment.

"You're frowning," he said. He slipped a hand around her neck and pulled her down until her face was within inches of his own. "Aren't you having a good time?"

She nodded, unable to deny the obvious.

"Then what's the problem?"

"Nothing."

He hesitated and the edges of his mouth lifted sensuously. "It's a good thing you decided against becoming an attorney," he said with a roguish grin. "You'd never be able to fool a jury."

Susannah was amazed that Nate knew she'd once seriously considered going into law.

"Don't look so shocked. Emily told me you'd thought about entering law school."

Susannah blinked a couple of times, then smiled. She brushed the hair from his brow, determined not to ruin this magnificent afternoon with her concerns.

"Kiss me, Susannah," he whispered. The humor had drained from his features and his gaze searched hers.

Her breath caught. Her eyes lifted and she quickly glanced around. The park was crowded and children were everywhere.

"No," he said, bracing his hands against the sides of her face. "No fair peeking. I want you to kiss me no matter how many spectators there are."

"But—"

"If you don't kiss me, then I'll simply have to kiss you. And, honey, if I do, watch out because—"

Not allowing him to finish, she lowered her mouth enough to gently skim her lips over his. Even that small sample was enough to send the blood racing through her veins. Whatever magic quality this man had should be bottled and sold over the counter. Susannah knew she'd be the first one in line to buy it.

"Are you always this stingy?" he asked when she lifted her head.

"In public, yes."

His eyes were smiling once more and Susannah swore she could have drowned in his look. He exhaled, then leaped to his feet with an energy she had to envy.

"I'm starved," he announced, reaching out for her. Susannah slipped her hand in his and he pulled her to her feet. "But I hope you realize," he whispered close to her ear, wrapping his arm around her waist, "my appetite isn't for food. I'm crazy about you, Susannah Simmons. Eventually we're going to have to do something about that."

"I HOPE I'M NOT too early," Susannah said as she entered her sister's home on Capitol Hill. When Emily had called to invite her to Sunday dinner, she hadn't bothered to disguise her intention. Emily was dying to grill Susannah about her budding relationship with Nate Townsend. A week ago, Susannah would have found an excuse to get out of it. But after spending an entire Saturday with Nate, she was so confused that she was willing to talk matters out with her sister, who seemed so much more competent in dealing with male/female relationships.

"Your timing's perfect," Emily said, coming out of the kitchen to greet her. She wore a full-length skirt with a bib apron, and her long hair was woven into a single braid that fell halfway down the middle of her back.

"Here." Susannah handed her sister a bottle of chardonnay, hoping it was appropriate for the meal.

"How thoughtful," Emily murmured, leading her back into the kitchen. The house was an older one, built in the early forties, with a large family kitchen. The red linoleum counter top was crowded with freshly canned tomatoes. Boxes of jars were stacked against one corner of the floor along with a wicker basket filled with fresh sun-dried diapers. A rope of garlic dangled from above the sink and a row of potted plants lined the windowsill.

"Whatever you're serving smells wonderful."

"It's lentil soup."

Emily opened the oven and pulled out the rack, wadding up the skirt of her apron to protect her fingers. "I made a fresh apple pie this morning. Naturally I used organically grown apples so you don't need to worry."

"Oh, good." That hadn't been a major concern of Susannah's.

"Where's Michelle?" Both father and daughter were conspicuously absent.

Emily turned around looking mildly guilty, and Susannah realized that her sister had gone to some lengths to provide time alone with her. No doubt she was anxious to wring as much information about Nate from her as possible. Not that Susannah had a lot to tell.

"So how was your day in the park?"

Susannah took a seat on the stool and made herself comfortable for the upcoming inquisition. "Great. We had a wonderful time."

"You like Nate, don't you?"

Like was the understatement of the year. Contrary to every ounce of sense she possessed, Susannah was falling in love with her neighbor. It wasn't what she wanted, but she hadn't been able to stop herself.

"Yes, I like him," she answered after a significant pause.

Emily looked delighted by her admission. "I thought as much," she said, nodding profoundly. She pushed a stool next to Susannah and sat down. Emily's hands were rarely idle, and true to form, she reached for her crocheting.

"I'm waiting," Susannah said, growing impatient.

"For what?"

"For the lecture."

Emily cracked a knowing smile. "I was just gathering my thoughts. You were always the one who would evaluate things so well. I had such trouble and you aced every paper."

"School reports have very little to do with real life," Susannah reminded her. How much simpler it would be if she could just look up everything she needed to know about dealing with Nate in an encyclopedia.

"I knew that, but I wasn't sure you did."

Perhaps Susannah hadn't until she met Nate. "Emily," she said, her stomach muscles tightening, "I need to ask you something...important. How did you know you loved Robert? What was it that told you the two of you were meant to share your lives?" Susannah realized she was practically laying her cards faceup on the table, but she was past the point for word games. She wanted hard facts.

Her sister smiled softly and tugged at her ball of yarn before she responded. "I don't think you're going to like my answer," she murmured, frowning slightly. "It was the first time Robert kissed me."

Susannah nearly toppled from her perch on the chair, remembering her experience with Nate. "What happened?"

"We'd gone for a nature walk in the rain forest over on the Olympic Peninsula and had stopped to rest. Robert helped me remove my backpack, then he looked into my eyes and leaned over and kissed me." She sighed softly at the memory. "I don't think he intended to do it because he looked so shocked afterward."

"Then what happened?"

"Robert took off his own backpack and asked if I'd minded that he'd kissed me. Naturally I told him I rather liked it, and he sat down next to me and did it again—only this time it wasn't a peck on the lips but a full-blown kiss." Emily's shoulders sagged a little in a sigh. "The moment his lips touched mine I couldn't think, I couldn't breathe, I couldn't even move. When he finished I was trembling so much I thought something might be physically wrong with me."

"So would you say you felt ... electricity?"

"Exactly."

"And you never had with any of the other men you'd dated?"

"Never."

Susannah wiped a hand down her face. "You're right," she whispered. "I don't like your answer."

Emily paused in her crocheting long enough to glance at her. "Nate kissed you and you felt something?"

Susannah nodded. "I was nearly electrocuted."

"Oh, Susannah, you poor thing!" She gently patted her sister's hand. "You don't know what to do, do you?"

"No," she admitted, feeling wretched.

"You never expected to fall in love, did you?"

Slowly Susannah shook her head. And it couldn't be happening at a worse time. The promotion was going to be announced within the next week or so, and the entire direction of her life could be altered if she became involved with Nate. Only she didn't know if that was what either of them wanted. Susannah felt mystified by all that was going on in her life, which until a few short weeks ago had been so straightforward and uncluttered.

"Are you thinking of marriage?" Emily asked outright.

"Marriage," Susannah echoed weakly. It seemed the natural conclusion when two people were falling in love. She was willing to admit her feelings, but she wasn't completely confident Nate felt the same things she did. Nor was she positive that he was ready to leap into something as permanent as a lifelong commitment. She knew *she* wasn't, and the very thought of all this was enough to throw her into a tizzy.

"I don't... know about marriage," Susannah admitted. "We haven't discussed anything like that." The fact was they hadn't even talked about dating regularly.

"Trust me, if you leave it to Nate the subject of marriage will never come up. Men never want to talk about getting married. The topic is left entirely up to us women."

"Oh, come on—"

"No, it's true. From the time Eve slipped Adam the apple, we've been left with the burden of taming man, and it's never more difficult than when it comes to convincing one he should take a wife."

"But surely Robert wanted to get married?"

"Don't be silly. Robert's like every other man alive. I had to convince him this was what he wanted. Subtlety is the key, Susannah. In other words I chased Robert until he caught me." She stopped working her crochet hook long enough to laugh softly at her own wit.

From the time she first met her brother-in-law, Susannah had assumed he'd taken one look at her sister and dropped to his knees to propose. It had always seemed obvious to Susannah that they were meant for each other, far more obvious than it was that Nate was right for her.

"I don't know, Emily," she said on the tail end of a jagged sigh. "Everything is so confused in my mind. How could I possibly be so attracted to this man? It doesn't make any sense! Do you know what we did yesterday afternoon when we'd finished at the park?" She didn't wait for a response. "Nate brought over his Nintendo game and Super Mario Brothers cartridge, and we played video games. Me! I can't believe it even now. It was a pure waste of time."

"Did you have fun?"

That was a question Susannah wanted to avoid. She'd laughed until her stomach muscles hurt. They'd challenged each other to see who could achieve the better score, and then had done everything possible to sabotage each other.

Nate discovered a sensitive area behind her ear and took to kissing her there just when she was about to outscore him. Fair was fair, however, and Susannah soon discovered Nate had his own area of vulnerability. Without a qualm, she had used it against him, effectively disrupting his game. Soon they both forgot Nintendo and became far more interested in learning about each other.

"We had fun" was all Susannah was willing to admit.

"What about the kite flying?"

Her sister didn't know when to quit. "Then, too," she acknowledged reluctantly. "And at the baseball game Thursday, as well."

"He took you to a Mariners game . . . on Thursday? But they played in the middle of the afternoon. Did you actually leave the office?"

Susannah nodded, without explaining the details of how Nate had practically kidnapped her. "Back to you and Robert," she said, wanting to change the subject.

"You want to know how I convinced him he wanted to get married? Actually, it wasn't so difficult."

For Emily it wouldn't have been, but for Susannah it would be another story entirely. The biggest problem was that she wasn't sure she wanted Nate to be convinced. However, she should probably know these things for future reference, and Emily was so much wiser in such matters. She'd listen to what her sister had to say and make up her mind later.

"Remember that old adage—the way to a man's heart is through his stomach? It's true. Men equate food with comfort and love—that's a well-known fact."

"I'm in trouble," Susannah announced flatly. Good grief, she thought, Nate could cook far better than she could any day of the week. If she couldn't attract him with her home-style cooking, then all she had in the way of looks was her classic profile. As painful as it was to accept, men simply weren't attracted to her.

"Now don't overreact. Just because you can't whip up a five-course meal doesn't mean your life is over before it even starts."

"My married life is. I can't put together soup and a sandwich and you know it."

"Susannah, I wish you'd stop demeaning yourself. You're bright and pretty, and Nate would be the luckiest man alive if he were to marry you."

Now that they were actually discussing marriage, Susannah was having mixed feelings. "I . . . don't know if Nate's the marrying kind," she muttered. "For that matter, I don't know if I am, either."

Emily ignored that. "I'll start you out on something simple and we'll work our way forward."

"Something simple. I don't understand."

"Cookies," Emily explained. "There isn't a man alive who doesn't appreciate homemade cookies. There's something magical about them—really," she added when Susannah cast her a doubtful glance. "Cookies create an aura of domestic bliss—I know it sounds crazy, but it's true. A man can't resist a woman who bakes him cookies. They remind him of home and mother and a warm fire crackling in the fireplace." Emily paused and sighed. "Now, it's also true that men have been fighting this feeling since the beginning of time.''

''What feeling?''

Emily glared at her. ''Domestic contentment. It's exactly what they need and want, but they fight it.''

Susannah mulled over her sister's words. ''Now that you mention it, Nate did say something about chocolate chip being his favorite.''

''See what I mean?''

Susannah couldn't believe she was pursuing this subject with her sister. Okay, so she and Nate shared some fun times. Lots of people had good times together. She was also willing to admit there was a certain amount of chemistry between them. But that wasn't any reason to run to the nearest altar.

For the past several minutes, she'd been trying to sensibly discuss this situation between Nate and her with her sister, and before she even knew how it happened, Emily had her talking about marriage and baking chocolate chip cookies. At this rate Emily would have her married and pregnant by the end of the week.

''So how did dinner go with your sister?'' Nate asked her later that same night. He'd been down on the Seattle waterfront earlier in the day and had brought her back a polished glass paperweight made of ash from the Mount St. Helens volcano.

''Dinner was fine,'' she said quickly, perhaps too quickly. ''Emily and I had a good talk.''

Nate wrapped his arms around her, trapping her against the kitchen counter. ''I missed you.''

Swallowing tensely, she exhaled and murmured, "I missed you, too."

He threaded his fingers though the length of her hair, pulling it away from her face and holding it there. "You wore it down again today," he whispered against her neck.

"Yes . . . Emily says she liked it that way better, too." Talking shouldn't be this difficult, but it was every time Nate touched her. Susannah's knees had the consistency of pudding and her resolve was just as weak. After analyzing her talk with Emily, Susannah had decided to let matters cool between her and Nate for a while. Things were happening much too quickly. She wasn't ready, and she doubted that Nate was, either.

When he kissed her lightly at the scented hollow of her throat, it was all she could do to remain in an upright position. As she braced her hands against his chest, she began to push him gently away and escape. But when his lips traveled up the side of her neck, blazing a trail of moist kisses, she was lost. His mouth grazed along the line of her jaw, slowly edging its way toward her lips, prolonging the inevitable until Susannah thought she would dissolve at his feet.

When he finally kissed her mouth, they both sighed, caught in a swelling tide of longing. His mouth moved hungrily over hers. Then he tugged at her lower lip with his teeth, creating a whole new wave of sensations.

By the time Nate returned to his apartment, Susannah was shaking from the inside out. She'd walked all the way to the kitchen before she realized her intent. She stared at the phone for a long moment. Calling Emily demanded every ounce of courage she possessed. With a deep calming breath, she punched out her sister's number.

"Emily," she said when her sister answered on the second ring, "do you have a recipe for chocolate chip cookies?"

CHAPTER SEVEN

THE RECIPE for chocolate chip cookies was safely tucked away in a kitchen drawer. The impulse to bake them had passed almost immediately and cool reason had returned.

Monday morning, back at the office, Susannah realized how close she'd come to the edge of insanity. The vice presidency was almost within her grasp, and she'd worked too long and too hard to let a promotion of this importance slip through her fingers simply because she felt a little weak in the knees when Nate Townsend kissed her. To even contemplate anything beyond friendship was like...like amputating her right hand because she had a sliver in her index finger. She'd been overreacting, which was understandable, since she'd never before experienced such a strong attraction to a man.

"There's a call for you on line one," Ms Brooks told her. Her secretary paused, then added dryly, "It sounds like that nice young man who stopped by last week."

Nate. Squaring her shoulders—and her resolve—Susannah picked up the phone. "This is Susannah Simmons."

"Good morning, beautiful."

"Hello, Nate," she said stiffly. "What can I do for you?"

He chuckled. "That's a leading question if there ever was one. Trust me, honey, you don't want to know."

"Nate," she breathed, briefly closing her eyes. "Please. I'm busy. What do you want?"

"Other than your body?"

Hot color leaped into her cheeks and she gave a distressed gasp. "I think we'd better put an end to this conversation—"

"All right, all right, I'm sorry. I just woke up and was lying here thinking how nice it would be if we could escape for the day. Could I tempt you with a drive to the ocean? We could dig for clams, build a sand castle, and then make a fire and sing our favorite camp songs."

"As a matter of interest, I've been up for several hours. And since you've obviously forgotten, I do have a job—an important one. At least it's important to me. Now exactly what is the purpose of this call, other than to embarrass me?"

"Lunch."

"I can't today. I've got an appointment."

"Okay." He sighed, clearly frustrated. "How about dinner, just you and me?"

"I'm working late and was planning on sending out for something. Thanks, anyway."

"Susannah," he said in a burst of impatience, "are we going to go through this again? You should know by now that avoiding me won't change anything."

Perhaps not, she reasoned, but it would certainly help. "Listen, Nate, I really am busy. Perhaps we should continue this conversation another time."

"Like next year—I know you. You'd be willing to bury your head in the sand for the next fifteen years if I didn't come and prod you along. I swear, I've never known a more stubborn woman."

"Goodbye, Nate."

"Susannah," he persisted, "what about dinner? Come on, change your mind. We have a lot to talk about."

"No. I wasn't lying—I do have to work late. The fact is, I can't go outside and play today—or tonight."

"Ouch," Nate cried. "That hurt."

"Perhaps it hit too close to home."

A short silence followed. "Maybe it did," he murmured thoughtfully. "But before we hang up, I do want to know when I can see you again."

Susannah leaned forward and stretched her arm across the desk to her calendar, flipping the pages until she found a blank space. "How about lunch on Thursday?"

"All right," he said, "I'll see you Thursday at noon."

For a long moment after they'd hung up, Susannah kept her hand on the receiver. As crazy as it seemed, spending the afternoon with Nate at the beach sounded far too appealing. The way he made her think and feel was almost frightening. The man was putting her entire career in jeopardy. Something had to be done, only Susannah wasn't sure what.

An hour later, Ms Brooks tapped gently on her door and walked inside, carrying a huge bouquet of red roses. "These just arrived."

"For me?" Surely there was some mistake. No one had ever sent her flowers before. There'd never been any reason. There wasn't now.

"The card has your name on it," her secretary informed her. She found the small white envelope and handed it to Susannah.

Not until her assistant had left the room did Susannah read the card. The roses were from Nate, who wrote that he was sorry for having disturbed her earlier. She was right, he told her, now wasn't the time to go outside and play. He'd signed it with his love. Closing her eyes, Susannah held the card to her breast and battled down a swelling surge of emotion. The least he could do was stop being so damn wonderful. Then everything would be so much easier.

As it turned out, Susannah finished relatively early that evening and returned home a little after seven. Her apartment was dark and empty—but it was that way every night and she didn't understand why it should matter to her now. Yet it did.

It wasn't until she stood outside Nate's front door and knocked that she realized how impulsive her behavior had become since she'd met him. She was doing everything within her power to avoid him, and at the same time she couldn't stay away.

"Susannah," he said when he opened the door. "This is a pleasant surprise."

She laced her fingers together. "I...I just wanted you to know how much I appreciated the roses. They're lovely and the gesture was so thoughtful."

"Come in," he said, stepping inside. "I'll put on some coffee."

"No, thanks. I've got to get back, but I just wanted to thank you for the flowers...and to apologize if I sounded waspish on the phone. Monday mornings aren't exactly my best time."

Grinning, he leaned against the doorjamb and crossed his arms over his broad chest. "Actually, I was the one who owed you an apology. I should never have phoned you this morning. I was being selfish and thoughtless. You do have an important job and these are anxious days for you. Didn't you tell me that you'd hear about that promotion within the next week or two?''

Susannah nodded.

''You might find this hard to believe, but I don't want to say or do anything that would take that away from you. You're a dedicated, hardworking employee and you deserve to be the first female vice president of H&J Lima.''

His confidence in her was reassuring, but confusing. From everything she'd witnessed about Nate, the last thing he appreciated was hard work and its rewards.

''If I do get that promotion,'' she said, watching him closely, ''things will change between you and me. I . . . I won't have a lot of free time for a while.''

''Does this mean you won't be able to go outside and play as often?'' he asked, his mouth curving into a sensuous smile. He was taunting her with the words she'd used earlier that morning.

''Exactly.''

''I can accept that. Just . . .'' He hesitated.

''What?'' Nate was frowning and that wasn't like him. He wore a saucy grin as often as he donned a baseball cap. ''Tell me,'' she demanded.

''I want you to do everything possible to achieve your dreams, Susannah, but there are plenty of pitfalls along the way you need to watch for.''

Now it was her turn to frown. She wasn't sure she understood what he was talking about.

''All I'm saying,'' he elaborated, ''is that you shouldn't lose sight of who you are because this vice presidency means so much to you. And even more important, count the cost.'' With that he stepped forward, gazed hungrily into her eyes and then kissed her lightly on the lips. Reluctantly he stepped back.

For a second Susannah teetered, then she moved forward into his arms as if that was the most natural place in the world for her to be. Even now, she wasn't entirely sure she understood what he was talking about, but she couldn't mistake the tenderness she heard in his voice. Once her head had cleared and she wasn't wrapped up in this incredible longing he created every time he touched her, she'd mull over his words.

SUSANNAH WOKE around midnight, and rolling over, adjusted her pillow. The illuminated dial on her clock radio told her she'd only been sleeping for a couple of hours. She yawned, wondering what had woken her out of a sound peaceful slumber. Closing her eyes, she tucked the blankets more securely over her shoulder, determined to sleep. She tried visualizing herself accepting the promotion to the vice presidency. Naturally, there'd be a nice write-up about her in the evening paper and possibly a short piece in the business journal.

Susannah's eyes drifted open as she recalled Nate's words reminding her not to forget who she was. Who was she? A list of possible replies skipped easily through her mind. She was Susannah Simmons, future vice president in charge of marketing for the largest sporting-goods store in the country. She was a daughter, a sister, an aunt... And then it hit her, hard between the eyes. *She was a woman*. That was what Nate had been trying to tell her. It was the same message Emily had struggled to get across to her on Sunday. From the time Susannah had set her goals, she'd dedicated her life to her career and pushed every feminine part of herself aside. Now was the time for her to deal with that aspect of her life.

IT WAS THE FOLLOWING EVENING after work. Susannah was leaning against the kitchen counter, struggling to remove the heavy food mixer from its reinforced cardboard box. The way she figured it, Emily's recipe for chocolate chip cookies made three dozen. After her trip to the grocery store, followed by a jaunt to the hardware store for the mixer, cookie sheets and measuring utensils, the cookies were costing her $4.72— each.

The price be damned. She was setting out to prove something important—although she wasn't sure exactly what! She'd have preferred to dismiss all her sister's talk about cookies being equated with warmth and love as a philosophy left over from an earlier generation. Susannah didn't actually believe Emily's theory, but still, she wanted to give it a try. Perhaps she wanted to prove something to herself. Susannah wasn't sure anymore. All she knew was that she had this incredible urge to bake chocolate chip cookies.

Emily had eagerly given her this recipe, and once Susannah thought about it, just how difficult could baking cookies be?

Not hard, she determined twenty minutes later when everything was laid out on her extended counter. Pushing up the sleeves of her shirt, she turned on the radio to keep her company. Next she tried the arms of an old shirt around her waist, using that as an apron. Emily always seemed to wear one when she worked in the kitchen and if her sister did, then it must be important.

The automatic mixer was blending the butter and white sugar nicely and, feeling extraordinarily proud of herself, Susannah cracked the eggs on the edge of the bowl with flair a French chef would have envied.

"Damn," she cried when half the shell fell into the swirling blades. She glared at it a moment, watching helplessly as the beater broke the fragile shell into a thousand pieces. Shrugging, she decided a little extra protein—or was it calcium?—wasn't going to hurt anyone. Finally she turned off the mixer and stirred in the flour, then the chocolate chips.

The oven was preheated exactly as the recipe required when Susannah slipped the shiny new cookie sheet inside. She closed the oven door with a swing of her hip and set the timer for twelve minutes.

Sampling a bite of the dough from the end of her finger, she had to admit it was downright tasty. At least as good as Emily's and perhaps even a little better. But Susannah considered it best not to let anyone know her secret ingredient was eggshell.

Feeling exceptionally proud at how easy everything had been, she poured herself a cup of coffee and sat down at the table with the evening paper.

It was a few minutes later that she smelled smoke. Suspiciously sniffing the air, she set the paper aside. It couldn't possibly be her cookies—they'd been in the oven less than five minutes. To be on the safe side, however, she reached for a pot holder and opened the oven door.

Immediately she was assaulted by billowing waves of smoke, followed by flames that licked out at her. Gasping in horror, she dropped the pot holder and gave a piercing scream. "Fire! Fire!"

The smoke alarm started ringing, and she swore she'd never heard anything louder in her life. Like a madwoman, Susannah raced for the door, throwing it open in an effort to allow the smoke to escape. Then she ran back to the table and hurled the liquid from her coffee cup straight into the belly of the oven. Coughing hoarsely, she slammed the door shut.

"Susannah!" Breathless, Nate burst into her condominium.

"I started a fire," she shouted above the deafening din of the smoke alarm. Her voice still sounded raspy.

"Where?" Nate circled her table several times, looking frantically for the source of her panic.

"In the oven." Standing aside, she covered her face with her hands, not wanting to look.

A few moments later, Nate took her in his arms. Two blackened sheets of charred cookies were angled into the sink. "Are you all right?"

Somehow she managed a nod.

"You didn't burn yourself?"

She didn't have so much as a blister and told him so.

Gently he brushed the hair away from her face, and expelled his breath in a long drawn-out exercise, apparently to ease his tension. "Okay, how did the fire get started?"

"I don't know," she said dismally. "I . . . I did everything the way the recipe said, but when I put them in the oven they...they started on fire." By this time her voice was wobbling, like the spin cycle in a washing machine that wasn't balanced.

"The cookies weren't responsible for the fire," he corrected. "The cookie sheets were the culprits. They must have been new—it seems, ah, you forgot to remove the paper covering from the backs."

"Oh," she whispered and the word escaped on a hiccuping sob. Her shoulders were shaking with the effort to repress her shudders.

"Susannah, there isn't any reason to cry. It was a reasonable mistake. Here, sit down." Gently he lowered her onto the kitchen chair and knelt in front of her, taking her hands in his and rubbing them. "It isn't the biggest disaster in the world."

"I know that," she wailed, unable to stop herself. "You don't understand. It was sort of a test...."

"A test?"

"Yes. Emily claims men love cookies...and I was baking them for you." She didn't go on to add that Emily also claimed that men loved the women who baked those cookies. "I can't cook...I started a fire...and I dropped part of the eggshell in the batter and...and left it.... I wasn't going to tell anyone."

Her confession must have shocked Nate because he stood up and left the room. Burying her face in her hands, Susannah struggled to regain her composure and was doing an admirable job of it when Nate returned, holding a box of tissue.

Effortlessly lifting her into his arms, he pulled out the chair and sat down, holding her securely on his lap. "Okay, Betty Crocker, explain yourself."

She wiped her face dry with the tissue, feeling rather silly at the way she was reacting. So she'd burned a couple of cookie sheets and ruined a batch of chocolate chip cookies. Big deal, she told herself with as much bravado as she could muster. "Explain what?"

"The comment about men loving cookies. Were you trying to prove something to me?"

"Actually it was Emily I wanted to set straight," she whispered.

"You said you were baking them for my benefit."

"I was. You mentioned something yesterday about me not forgetting who I was, finding myself and

I . . . think this sudden urge to bake was my response to that. Believe me, after today, I know I'm never going to be worth a tinker's damn in the kitchen.''

"I don't remember suggesting you 'find yourself' in the kitchen,'' Nate said, looking confused.

"Actually that part was Emily's idea,'' she admitted. "She's the one who gave me the recipe. My sister seems to believe a woman can coerce a man into selling his heart and soul if she can bake chocolate chip cookies.''

"And you want my heart and soul?''

"Of course not! Don't be ridiculous.''

He hesitated for a moment and seemed to be considering her words. "Would it come as a surprise if I said I wanted yours?''

Susannah barely heard him; she wasn't in the mood to talk about heart and soul now. She'd just proved how worthless she was in the kitchen. Her lack in that area hadn't particularly troubled her until now. She'd made a genuine effort and fallen flat on her face. Not only that, to have Nate witness her defeat had badly dented her pride. "When I was born something must have been missing from my genes,'' she murmured thoughtfully. "Obviously. I can't cook, and I don't sew, and I haven't got the foggiest idea of how to tell one end of a knitting needle from the other. I can't do any of the things that . . . normal people associate with the female gender.''

"Susannah.'' He said her name on a disgruntled sigh. "Did you hear what I just said?''

In response, she shook her head. She understood everything perfectly. Some women had it and others didn't. Unfortunately, she was in the latter group.

"I was telling you something important. But I can see you're going to force me to say it without words." Cupping her face, Nate directed her mouth to his. But he didn't only kiss her this time. The hot moist tip of his tongue traced the sensitive line of her lips until she shivered with a whole new realm of unexplored sensations. All her disheartened thoughts dissolved instantly. She forgot to think, to breathe, to do anything but tremble in his arms. The fire in her oven was nothing compared to the one Nate started in her body. Without conscious thought, she wrapped her arms around his neck and slanted her mouth over his, surrendering to the hot currents of sensation he'd created. She opened herself to him, granting him anything he wanted. His tongue found hers, and Susannah whimpered at the shock of pleasure she received. The sound was absorbed by Nate. Her response, she realized, was innocent and abandoned, unskilled and unknowing, yet eager.

"There," he whispered, supporting his forehead against hers, while he sucked in deep breaths. His husky voice was unsteady.

He said it as if that was enough to prove everything. Susannah slowly opened her eyes. She drew in a steadying breath herself, one that caused her to tremble all the way to her toes. If she was going to say anything, it would be to repeatedly whisper his name and ask him why he was doing this and then plead with him never to stop.

He threaded his fingers through her hair and kissed her again with a mastery that caused her to cling to him as if he were a life raft in a stormy sea. Unable to keep still, Susannah ran her palms against the sides of his neck and onto his shoulders and down the length of his arms. He must have liked her touch because he groaned and deepened the kiss even more.

"Unfortunately I don't think you're ready to hear it yet," he said softly.

"Hear what?" she asked, when she could find her voice.

"What I was telling you."

She puckered her brow. "What was that?"

"Forget the cookies. You're more than enough woman for any man."

She blinked, not understanding him. Lord, she barely understood herself.

"I never meant for you to test who you are. All I suggested was that you take care not to lose sight of your own personality. Goals are all well and good, even necessary, but you should calculate the cost."

"Oh." Her mind was still too hazy to properly assimilate his meaning.

"Are you going to be all right?" he asked, as he grazed her cheek with his fingertips. He kissed Susannah's eyelids, closing them.

It was all she could do to nod.

"JOHN HAMMER WOULD LIKE to see you right away," Ms Brooks told Susannah when she walked into her office Thursday morning.

Susannah's heart zoomed to her throat and stayed there for an uncomfortable moment. This was it. The day for which she'd been waiting five long years.

"Did he say what he wanted?" she asked, struggling to appear at least outwardly calm.

"No," Ms Brooks returned. "He just asked me to tell you he wanted to talk to you at your convenience."

Susannah slumped into the thick cushion of her high-backed office chair. She propped her elbows on the desk and buried her face in her hands, trying to put some order to her muddled thoughts. "At my convenience," she repeated in a ragged whisper. "I didn't get the promotion. I just know it."

"Susannah," her secretary said sternly, calling her by her first name—something she'd never done in the past. "I think you might be jumping to conclusions."

Susannah glared at her, annoyed by the woman's obtuseness. "If he planned to appoint me as vice president, he would have called me into his office late in the afternoon. That's the way it's always done. Then he'd go through this long spiel about me being a loyal employee and what an asset I am to the company and all that rot. Wanting to talk to me *now* means... Well, you know what it means."

"I can't say that I do," Ms Brooks said primly. "My suggestion is that you pull yourself together and get over to Mr. Hammer's office before he changes his mind."

Susannah got to her feet and stiffened her spine. Her stomach felt like a pot of melted honey, and no matter how hard she tried she couldn't seem to stop shaking.

"I'll be waiting here when you get back," Ms Brooks told her on her way out the door. She smiled then, an encouraging gesture that softened her austere features. "Break a leg, kid."

"I think I will, whatever happens." If she didn't get this promotion, she was afraid she'd fall apart. Forcing a calm manner, she decided not to worry until she knew for sure.

John Hammer stood up when she was announced. Susannah walked into his office, and the first thing she noticed was that the two men who were her competition hadn't been called. The company president smiled benignly and motioned toward a chair. Susannah sat on the edge of the cushion, doing her best to disguise how nervous she was.

A smile eased over her employer's features. "Good morning, Susannah . . ."

True to her word, Susannah's secretary was waiting for her when she strolled back to her office.

"Well?"

Eleanor Brooks followed her to her desk and watched as Susannah carefully sat down.

"What happened?" she demanded a second time. "Don't just sit there. Talk."

Susannah's gaze slowly moved from the phone to her secretary. Then she started to chuckle. The laughter came from deep within her chest and she had to cover her mouth with her palms. When she could talk, she wiped the tears from the corners of her eyes.

"The first thing he did was ask me if I wanted to trade offices while mine was being repainted."

"What?"

Susannah thought Ms Brooks's look probably reflected her own when Mr. Hammer had asked that question. "That was my first reaction, too," Susannah exclaimed. "I didn't understand what he meant. Then he said he was going to have my office done, because he thought it was only right that the vice president in charge of marketing have a brand new office.

"You got the promotion?" Eleanor Brooks clapped her hands in sheer delight, then pressed them over her lips.

"I got it," Susannah breathed, squeezing her eyes shut. "I actually got it."

"Congratulations."

"Thank you, thank you." Already she was reaching for the phone. She had to tell Nate. Only a few days before he had said she should go after her dreams, and less than two days later everything was neatly falling into place.

There was no answer at his apartment and, dejected, she replaced the receiver. The need to talk to him consumed her, and she tried again every half hour until she thought she'd go crazy.

At noon, she was absorbed in her work when her secretary announced that her luncheon date had arrived.

"Send him in," Susannah said automatically, irritated that her concentration had been broken.

Casually Nate strolled into her office and plopped himself down in the chair opposite her desk.

"Nate," she cried, leaping to her feet. "I've been trying to get hold of you all morning. What are you doing here?"

"We're going out to lunch, remember?"

CHAPTER EIGHT

"NATE." SUSANNAH RAN around her desk until she stood directly in front of him. "John Hammer called me into his office this morning," she explained breathlessly. "I got the promotion. You're looking at the vice president in charge of marketing for H&J Lima."

For a moment Nate said nothing. Then he asked slowly, thoughtfully, as if he wasn't sure he'd heard her correctly, "You got the promotion?"

"Yes," she repeated. "I got it."

"You actually got it." Nate's eyes were wide with awe.

In her enthusiasm, Susannah nodded several times, with a violence that seemed to dislocate her neck. She was smiling so hard, her face ached.

Throwing back his head, Nate let out a shout that must have shaken the ceiling tile. Then he locked his arms around her waist, lifted her from the floor and swung her around, all the while howling with delight.

Susannah threw back her head and laughed with him. She'd never experienced a moment of joy more profoundly. The promotion hadn't seemed real to her until she had shared it with Nate. The first person she'd thought to tell had been him. He had become the very center of her world, and it was time to admit she was in love with him.

Nate had stopped whirling her around, but he continued to grip her middle so that her face was elevated above his own.

Breathless with happiness, Susannah smiled down on him and on impulse she buried her fingers in his hair. She couldn't resist him, not now, when she was filled with such exhilaration. Her mouth was trembling when she kissed him. She made a soft throaty sound of discovery and pleasure, then lifted her head and smiled at him, noticing how deep and blue his eyes were. Her gaze lowered to the sensual lines of his mouth, and she remembered how she'd felt when he'd held and reassured her after the cookie disaster. She lowered her lips once more, lightly rocking her head back and forth, creating a friction that was so hot, she felt as though she'd catch fire.

In an unhurried movement, Nate lowered her to the ground and wrapped his arms around her. "Susannah," he moaned, kissing the corner of her mouth with exquisite care, "the things you do to me."

With a shudder, she opened her mouth to him. She wanted him to kiss her the way he had in the past. Deep, slow, moist, kisses that made her forget to breathe. She yearned for the taste and scent of him to fill her so she couldn't tell where she ended and he began. This was the happiest moment of her life, and only a small portion could be attributed to the promotion. Everything else was Nate and the mounting love she felt for him each time they were together.

Someone coughed nervously in the background, and Nate broke off the kiss and stared impatiently past her to the open door.

"Ms Simmons," her secretary said, smiling broadly.

"Yes?" Breaking away from Nate, Susannah smoothed the hair at the sides of her head and struggled to replace her business facade.

"I'll be leaving now. Ms Andrews will be answering your calls."

"Thank you, Ms Brooks," Nate muttered, but there was little appreciation in his tone.

Susannah chastised him with a look. "We'll...I'll be leaving directly for my luncheon appointment."

"I'll tell Ms Andrews."

"This afternoon, I'd like you to call a meeting of the staff," Susannah said, "and I'll announce the promotion."

Eleanor Brooks nodded, but her smiling eyes landed heavily on Nate. "I believe everyone has already guessed from the...commotion that came from here a few minutes ago."

"I see." Susannah couldn't help smiling.

"There isn't an employee here who isn't happy about your news."

"I can think of two," Susannah said under her breath, remembering the men she'd been competing against. Nate squeezed her hand, and it was all she could do to keep from laughing outright.

Her assistant closed the door on her way out, and the minute she did, Nate reached for Susannah to bring her back into the shelter of his arms. "Where were we?"

"About to leave for lunch, as I recall."

Nate frowned. "That's not the way I remember it."

Susannah laughed and squeezed him tightly, loving him all the more. "I think we both forgot ourselves." She broke away and reached for her purse, hooking the long strap over her shoulder. "Are you ready?"

"Any time you are." But the hot eager look in his eyes told her he was talking about something other than lunch.

Susannah could feel the color working its way up her neck and suffusing her face. "Nate," she whispered, lowering her gaze, "behave yourself. Please."

"I'm doing the best I can under the circumstances," he whispered back, his eyes filled with mischievous delight. "In case you haven't figured it out yet, I'm crazy about you, woman."

"I . . . I'm pretty keen on you myself."

"Good." He tucked his arm around her waist and led her out of the office and down the long hallway to the elevator. Susannah was certain she could feel the stares of her staff members, but for the first time, she didn't care what image she projected. Everything was right in her world, and she'd never been happier.

Nate chose the restaurant, Il Bistro, which was one of the best in town. The atmosphere was festive, and playing the role of the gentleman to the hilt, Nate wouldn't so much as allow her to look at the menu, insisting that he'd order for her.

"Nate," she whispered once the waiter had left the table, "I want to pay for this. It's a business lunch."

His thick brows arched upward. "And how are you going to rationalize that when your boss questions you about it, my dear?" He wiggled his eyebrows suggestively.

"There's a reason I agreed to go to lunch with you—other than celebrating my promotion, which was something I didn't even know about until this morning." As she'd explained to Nate earlier, her life was going to change with this promotion. New responsibility would result in a further commitment of time and energy to the company, and could drastically alter her relationship with Nate. If anything, she wanted them to grow closer, not apart. This advancement had the potential to make or break them, and Susannah was looking for a way to draw them closer together. She thought she'd found it.

"A reason?" Nate questioned.

They were interrupted by the waiter as he produced a bottle of expensive French wine for their inspection. He removed the cork and poured a sample into the glass for Nate to taste. When Nate nodded in approval, the waiter filled their glasses and discreetly retreated.

"Now, you were saying?" Nate continued, studying her. His mouth quirked up at the edges.

Gathering her resolve, Susannah reached across the table and gripped Nate's hand. "You've always been open and honest with me. I want you to know how much I appreciate that. When I asked you if you had a job, you admitted you'd had one until recently and that you'd quit." She waited for him to elaborate on his circumstances, but he didn't, so she went on. "It's obvious you don't need the money, but there's something else, just as important, that's obvious, too."

Nate removed his fingers from hers and twirled the stem of the wineglass between his open palms. "What's that?"

"You lack purpose."

His gaze lifted to meet hers and his brow creased in query.

"You have no direction," she announced flatly. "Over the past several weeks, I've watched you flit from one area of interest to another. First it was baseball, then it was video games, then kite flying, and tomorrow, no doubt, it'll be something else."

"Traveling," he concluded for her. "I was thinking of doing some serious sight-seeing. I have a hankering to stroll the byways of Hong Kong."

"Hong Kong," she repeated, gesturing with her hands. "That's exactly what I mean." Her heart slowed to a sluggish beat at the thought of his being gone for any length of time. She'd become accustomed to having Nate close, to sharing bits and pieces of her day with him. Not only had she fallen in love with him, he'd quickly become her best friend.

"Do you think traveling is wrong?" he asked.

"Not wrong," she returned swiftly. "But what are you going to do once you've run out of ways to entertain yourself and places to travel? What are you going to do when you've spent all your money?"

"I'll face that when the time comes."

"I see." She lowered her gaze, wondering if she was only making matters worse. There was little she could say to counter his don't-worry attitude.

"Susannah, you make it sound like the end of the world. Trust me, wealth isn't all that great. If I run out of money, fine. If I don't, that's all right, too."

"I see," she murmured miserably.

"You claimed you understood a few minutes ago," he countered with a smile. "How can you *see* again so soon?"

"It's because I care about you, I guess." She paused and drew in a deep breath. "We may live in the same building, but our worlds are totally different. My future is charted, right down the day I retire at age sixty-five. I know what I want and how to get there."

"I thought I did once, too, but then I learned how unimportant it all was."

"It doesn't have to be like that," she told him, her voice filled with determination. "Listen, there's something important I'm going to propose, but I don't want you to answer me now. I want you to give yourself time to think about it. Promise me you'll do at least that."

"Are you suggesting we get married?" he teased.

"No." Flustered, she smoothed out the linen napkin in her lap, her fingers lingering there to disguise her nervousness. "I'm offering you a job."

"You're doing what?" He half rose out of his seat.

Embarrassed, Susannah glanced nervously around her and noted that several people had stopped eating and were glancing in their direction. "Don't look so aghast. A job would make a lot of difference in your attitude toward life."

"And just exactly what position are you offering me?" Now that the surprise had worn off, he appeared amused.

"I don't know, at least not yet. We'd have to figure out something with personnel. But I'm sure that there would be a position open that would fit your qualifications."

The humor drained from his eyes, and for a long moment Nate said nothing. "You think a job would give me purpose?"

"I believe so." To her way of thinking, it would help him look beyond today and toward the future. Employment would lend Nate a reason to get out of bed in the mornings, instead of sleeping in until nine or ten every day.

"Susannah—"

"Before you say anything," she interrupted, holding up her hand, "I want you to think it over seriously.

Don't say anything until you've had a chance to consider my offer.''

His eyes were more serious than she could ever remember seeing them—other than just before he wanted to kiss her. His look was almost brooding.

Their meal arrived, and the lamb was as delicious as Nate had promised. He was unusually quiet during the remainder of the meal, but that didn't surprise her. He was reflecting on her job offer and that was exactly what she wanted. She hoped he'd come to the right decision. Loving him the way she did, she longed to make his world as right as her own.

Despite Nate's protests, Susannah paid for their lunch. He walked her back to her office, standing with her on the sidewalk while they exchanged a few words of farewell. Susannah kissed him on the cheek and asked once more that he consider her job offer.

''I will,'' he promised, lightly running his finger down the side of her face.

He left her then, and Susannah watched as he walked away, letting her gaze linger on him for several minutes.

''Any messages?'' she asked Dorothy Andrews, who was sitting in her secretary's place.

''One,'' Dorothy said, without looking up. ''Emily—she didn't leave her full name. She said she'd catch you later.''

''Thanks.'' Susannah took the pink slip into her office and, sitting down at her desk, punched out her sister's telephone number.

''Emily, this is Susannah. You phoned?''

''I know I probably shouldn't have called you at the office, but you never seem to be home and I had something important to ask you," her sister said, talking so fast she ran her words together.

"What's that?" Already Susannah was reaching for a file, intending to read while her sister spoke. It sometimes took Emily several minutes to get around to the purpose of any call.

Her sister hesitated. "I've got several large zucchini left from my garden, and I was wondering if you wanted one."

"About as much as I want a migraine headache." After her disaster with the chocolate chip cookies, Susannah planned never to so much as read a recipe again.

"The zucchini are excellent this time of year," Emily prompted, as if that would be enough to induce Susannah into agreeing to take a truckload.

Her sister hadn't phoned her to ask about zucchini, Susannah would have staked her promotion on it. The Italian vegetable was a lead-in for something else, and no doubt it would be left to Susannah to play a guessing game. Mentally, she scanned a list of possible favors and decided to leap in with both feet.

"Zucchini are out, but I wouldn't mind taking care of Michelle again, if you need me."

"Oh, Susannah, would you? I mean, it'd work out so great if you could keep her two weeks from this Saturday."

"All night?" As much as she loved her niece, another overnight stretch was more than Susannah wanted to contemplate. As it was, Nate would probably be more than happy to lend a hand. No doubt she'd need it.

"Oh, no, not for the night, just for dinner. Robert's boss is taking us out to eat, and it wouldn't be appropriate if we took Michelle along. Robert got a big promotion, did I tell you?''

''No.''

''I'm so proud of him. I think he's probably the best accountant in Seattle.''

Susannah toyed with the idea of letting her sister in on her own big news, but she didn't want to take anything away from her brother-in-law. She could let them both know in two weeks when they dropped off Michelle.

''I'll be happy to keep Michelle for you,'' Susannah said, and discovered, as she marked the date on her calendar, how much she actually meant that. She might be a disaster waiting to happen in the kitchen, but she didn't do half badly with her niece. The time might yet come when she'd seriously consider having a child or two of her own—not now, of course, but sometime in the future. ''All right, I've got you down for the seventeenth.''

''Susannah, I can't tell you how much this means to me,'' Emily said.

BY THE TIME Susannah arrived home that evening she was tipsy. The staff meeting that afternoon had gone wonderfully well. After five, she'd been taken out for a drink by her two top aides, to celebrate. Several others from her section had unexpectedly dropped by the cocktail lounge and insisted on buying her drinks too. By seven, Susannah was flushed and excited, and from experience, she knew it was time to call it quits and phone for a taxi.

Dinner probably would have cut the effects of the alcohol, but she was more interested in getting home.

After a nice hot bath, she'd fix herself some toast and be done with it.

She hadn't been home more than a half hour when her phone rang. Dressed in her robe and sipping tea in the kitchen, she reached for the receiver.

"Susannah, it's Nate. Can I come over?"

Glancing down at her robe and fuzzy slippers, she decided it wouldn't take her long to change.

"Give me five minutes."

"All right."

Dressed in slacks and a sweater, she opened the door when he knocked. "Hi," she greeted cheerfully, aware her mouth had probably formed a crooked grin despite her efforts to smile naturally.

Nate barely looked at her. His hands were thrust deep in his pockets, and his expression was disgruntled as he marched into her apartment. He didn't take a seat but paced the carpet in front of her fireplace like a soldier on guard duty. Obviously something was going on.

She sat on the edge of the sofa, carefully watching him, feeling more than a little reckless and exhilarated from the promotion and the celebration that had followed. She was amused, too, at Nate's peculiar agitation.

"I suppose you want to talk to me about the job offer," she asked, surprised by how controlled her voice sounded.

He paused, splayed his fingers through his thick hair and nodded. "That's exactly what I want to talk about."

"Don't," she said, smiling up at him.

His brow puckered in a frown. "Why not?"

"Because I wanted you to give long and careful consideration to the proposal."

"I need to explain something to you first."

Susannah wasn't listening. There were far more important things she had to tell him. "You're personable, bright and attractive," she began enthusiastically. "You could be anything in the world that you wanted, Nate. Anything."

"Susannah..."

She waved a finger at him and shook her head. "There's something else you should know."

"What?" he demanded.

"I'm in love with you." Her glorious confession was followed by a loud yawn. Unnerved, she covered her mouth with the tips of her fingers. "Oops, sorry."

Nate's eyes narrowed suspiciously. "Have you been drinking?"

She pressed her thumb and index finger together and held them up for his inspection. "Just a little, but I'm more happy than anything else."

"Susannah!" He dragged her name out into the longest, most splendid sigh. "I can't believe you."

"Why not? Do you want me to shout it to all of Seattle, because I will. Watch!" She waltzed into the kitchen and jerked open the sliding glass door.

Actually, some of the effects of the alcohol had worn off, but she'd experienced this irrepressible urge to tell Nate how much she'd come to care for him. They'd skirted around the subject long enough. He didn't seem to want to admit it, but she was, especially now, fortified with her good fortune. This day had been one of the most fantastic of her life. After years of hard work, everything was falling neatly into place, and she'd found the most wonderful man in the world to love—even if he *was* misguided.

The wind whipped against her on the balcony, and the multicolored lights from the waterfront below resembled those on a Christmas tree. Standing at the railing, she cupped her hands over her mouth and shouted, "I love Nate Townsend!" Satisfied, she whirled to face him and opened her arms as wide as they would go. "See? I just announced it to the world."

He joined her outside, and wrapped his arms around her and closed his eyes. Susannah had expected him to at least show some emotion.

"You don't look very happy about it," she challenged.

"You're not yourself."

"Then who am I?" Fists digging into her hips, she glared up at him, her eyes defiant. "I feel like me. I bet you think I'm drunk, but I'm not."

He didn't reply. Instead he threw an arm over her shoulder and urged her into the kitchen. Then, quickly and efficiently, he started to make coffee.

"I gave up caffeine," she announced.

"When was this? You had regular coffee today at lunch," he said.

"Just now." She giggled. "Come on, Nate," she cried, bending forward and snapping her fingers. "Loosen up a little."

"I'm more concerned about sobering you up."

"You could kiss me."

"I could," he admitted, "but I'm not going to."

"Why not?" She pouted, disappointed by his refusal.

"Because if I do, I may not be able to stop."

Sighing, she closed her eyes and heaved her shoulders. "That's the most romantic thing you've ever said to me."

Nate rubbed a hand over his face and leaned against the kitchen counter. "Have you had anything to eat since lunch?"

"One stuffed mushroom, a water chestnut wrapped in a slice of bacon and a piece of celery filled with something cheesy."

"But no dinner?"

"I was going to make myself some toast, but I wasn't hungry."

"After a stuffed mushroom, a celery stick and a water chestnut? I can see why not."

"Are you trying to be cute with me? Oh, just a minute, there was something I was supposed to ask you." She pulled herself up short and covered one eye, while she tugged at her memory for the date her sister had mentioned. "Are you doing anything on the seventeenth?"

"The seventeenth? Why?"

"Michelle's coming over to visit her Auntie Susannah and I know she'll want to see you, too."

Nate looked even more disturbed, but he hadn't seemed particularly pleased about anything from the moment he'd arrived.

"I've got something else on that night."

"Oh, well, I'll make do. I have before." She stopped abruptly. "No, I guess I haven't, but Michelle and I'll be just fine, I think..."

The coffee had finished dripping through into the glass pot. Nate poured a cup and, scowling, handed it to her.

"Oh, Nate, what's wrong with you? You haven't been yourself since you arrived. We should be kissing by now and all you seem to do is ignore me."

"Drink your coffee."

He stood over her until she'd taken the first sip. She grimaced at the heat. "You know what I drank tonight? I've never had them before and they tasted so good. Shanghai Slungs."

"They're called Singapore Slings."

"Oh." Maybe she was more confused than she thought.

"Come on, drink up, Tokyo Rose."

Obediently Susannah did as he requested. The whole time she was sipping away at her coffee, she was watching Nate, who moved restlessly about her kitchen, as if unable to stand still. He was disturbed by something, and she wished she knew what.

"Done," she announced when she'd finished, pleased with herself and this minor accomplishment. "Nate," she said, growing concerned, "do you love me?"

He paused and turned around to face her, his eyes serious. "So much I can't believe it myself."

"Oh, good," she said with an expressive sigh. "I was beginning to wonder."

"Where are your aspirin?" He was searching through her cupboards, opening and closing the ones closest to the sink.

"My aspirin? Did telling me how you feel give you a headache?"

"No." He turned and answered her with a gentle smile. "I want to have it ready for you in the morning because you're going to need it."

Her love for him increased tenfold. "You are so good to me!"

"Take two tablets first thing when you wake up and that should help a little." He crouched in front of her and took both her hands in his. "I'm leaving tomor-

row and I won't be back for a couple days. I'll call you,
all right?''

"You're going away to think about the job I offered
you, aren't you? That's a good idea—when you come
back you can tell me your decision." She was forced to
stop in order to yawn, a huge jaw-breaking yawn that
depleted her strength. "I think I should go to bed, don't
you?''

THE NEXT THING Susannah knew, her alarm was buzz-
ing angrily. With the sound came a piercing pain that
shot straight through her temple. She groped for the
clock, turned it off and sighed with relief. Sitting up in
bed proved to be equally overwhelming and she
groaned.

When she'd managed to maneuver herself into the
kitchen, she saw the aspirin bottle and remembered that
Nate had insisted on setting it out the night before.

"Bless that man," she said aloud and winced at the
sound of her own voice.

By the time she arrived at the office, she was operat-
ing on only three cylinders. Eleanor Brooks didn't seem
to be any better off than Susannah was. They took one
look at each other and smiled knowingly.

"Your coffee's ready," her secretary informed her.

"Did you have a cup yourself?''

"Yes.''

"Anything in the mail?''

"Nothing that can't wait. Mr. Hammer was in earlier. He told me to give you this magazine and said
you'd be as impressed as he was." Susannah glanced
over a six-year-old issue of *Business Monthly*, a trade
magazine that was highly respected in the industry.

"It's several years old," Susannah noted, wondering why her employer would want her to read it now.

"Mr. Hammer said there was a special feature in there about your friend."

"My friend?" Susannah didn't understand.

"Your friend," Eleanor Brooks repeated. "The one with the sexy eyes—Nathaniel Townsend."

CHAPTER NINE

SUSANNAH WAITED until her secretary had left the office before opening the magazine. The article on Nathaniel Townsend was the lead feature. The picture showed a much younger Nate standing in front of a shopping-mall outlet for Rainy Day Cookies, the most successful cookie chain in the country. In his hand he was holding a huge chocolate chip cookie.

Rainy Day Cookies were Susannah's absolute favorite. There were several varieties, but the chocolate chip ones were fantastic.

Two paragraphs into the article, Susannah thought she was going to be physically ill. She stopped reading and closed her eyes to the waves of nausea that lapped against her. Pressing a hand to her stomach, she resolutely focused her attention on the article, storing away the details of Nate's phenomenal success in her numb mind.

He had started his cookie company in his mother's kitchen while still in college. His specialty was chocolate chip cookies, and they were so popular that he soon found himself caught up in a fairy-tale roller-coaster ride that had led him straight to the top of the corporate world. By age twenty-eight, Nate Townsend was a multimillionaire.

Now that she thought about it, an article she'd read six or seven months ago in the same publication had

stated that the company was recently sold for an undis-
closed sum, which several estimated to be a figure so
staggering Susannah had gasped out loud.

Bracing her elbows on the desk, Susannah took several calming breaths. She'd made a complete idiot of
herself over Nate, and worse, he had let her. She suspected this humiliation would stay with her for the rest
of her life.

To think she'd baked the cookie king of the world
chocolate chip cookies, and in the process nearly set the
kitchen on fire. But that degradation couldn't compare
to yesterday's little pep talk when she'd spoken to him
about drive, ambition and purpose, before—dear
heaven, it was too much—she'd offered him a job. How
he must have laughed at that.

Eleanor Brooks brought in the mail and laid it on the
corner of Susannah's desk. Susannah glanced up at her
secretary and knew then and there that she wasn't going
to be able to cope with the business of the day.

"I'm going home."

Ms Brooks stopped abruptly. "I beg your pardon?"

"If anyone needs me, tell them I'm home sick."

"But..."

Susannah knew she'd shocked her assistant. In all the
years she'd been employed by H&J Lima, Susannah had
never used a single day of her sick leave. There'd been
a couple of times when she probably should have stayed
home, but she'd insisted on working anyway.

"I'll see you Monday morning," she announced on
her way out the door.

"I hope you're feeling better then."

"I'm sure I will be." She needed some time alone to
lick her wounds and gather the scattered pieces of her

pride. To think that only a few hours earlier she'd drunkenly declared her undying love to Nate Townsend!

That was the worst of it.

When Susannah walked into her apartment she felt as if she was stumbling into a bomb shelter. For the moment she was safe from the world outside. Eventually she'd have to go back and face it, but for now she was secure.

She picked up the afghan her sister had crocheted for her, wrapped it around her shoulders and sat staring sightlessly into space.

What an idiot she'd been! What a fool! Closing her eyes, she leaned her head against the back of the sofa and drew in several deep breaths, releasing the anger and hurt before it fermented into bitterness. She refused to allow her mind to dwell on the might-have-beens and the if-onlys, opting instead for a more positive approach. *Next time*, she would know enough not to involve her heart. *Next time*, she'd take care not to make such a fool of herself.

It amazed her when she awoke an hour later, to realize she'd fallen asleep. Tucking the blanket more securely around her, she analyzed her situation.

Things weren't so bad. She'd achieved her primary goal and was vice president in charge of marketing. The first female to hold such a distinguished position in the company's long history, she reminded herself. Her life was good. If on occasion she felt the yearning for a family of her own, there was always Emily, who was more than willing to share. Heaving a sigh, Susannah told herself that she lacked for nothing. She was respected, hardworking and healthy. Life was good.

Her head ached and her stomach didn't feel much better, but at noon, Susannah heated some chicken

noodle soup and forced that down. She was putting the
bowl in the dishwasher when the telephone rang. Ms
Brooks was the only one who knew she was home, and
her assistant would call her only if it was important.
Susannah answered the phone just as she would in her
office.

"Susannah Simmons."

"Susannah, it's Nate."

She managed to swallow a gasp. "Hello, Nate," she
said as evenly as possible. "What can I do for you."

"I called the office and your secretary said you'd
gone home sick."

"Yes. I guess I had more to drink last night than I
realized. I had one doozer of a hangover when I woke
up this morning." But she didn't add how her malady
had worsened once she read the article about him.

"Did you find the aspirin on the kitchen counter?"

"Yes. Now that I think about it, you were by last
night, weren't you?" She was thinking fast, wanting to
cover her tracks. "I suppose I made a fool of myself,"
she said, forcing a lightness into her tone. "I didn't say
anything to embarrass you . . . or me, did I?"

He chuckled softly. "You don't remember?"

She did, but she'd rather have been tortured than admit it. "Some of it, but most of the evening remains
fuzzy."

"Once I'm back in Seattle I'll help you recall every
single word." His voice was low, seductive and filled
with promise.

That was one guarantee, however, that Susannah had
no intention of accepting.

"I...probably made a complete idiot of myself," she
mumbled. "If I were you, I'd forget anything I said.
Obviously, I can't be held responsible for it."

"Susannah, Susannah, Susannah," Nate said gently. "Let's take this one step at a time."

"I...think we should talk about this later, I really do...because it's all too obvious I wasn't myself." Moisture pooled at the corners of her eyes and poured down her face. Furious at this display of emotion, she wiped the tears aside with the back of her hand.

"You're feeling better now?"

"Yes...no. I was just about to lie down."

"Then I'll let you," Nate said. "I'll be back Sunday. My flight should arrive early afternoon. I'd like us to have dinner together."

"Sure," she said, without thinking, willing to agree to just about anything in order to put an end to this conversation. She was still too raw, still bleeding. By Sunday, she'd be able to handle the situation far more effectively without all this emotion. By Sunday, she could disguise her pain.

"I'll see you around five then."

"Sunday," she echoed, feeling like a robot programmed to do exactly as its master requested. She had no intention of having dinner with Nate, none whatsoever. He'd find out why soon enough.

The only way Susannah made it through Saturday was by working. She stopped off at her office and sorted through the mail Ms Brooks had left on her desk. News of her promotion was to be announced in the Sunday business section of the *Seattle Times*, but word had apparently already leaked out, probably through her boss; a speaking invitation was in the mail, for a luncheon at a conference of local salespeople who had achieved a high level of success. The request was an honor and Susannah scribbled off a note of acceptance to the organizer. She considered it high praise to have been asked. The date of the conference was the seventeenth, which was only two weeks away, so she spent a good portion of the morning typing up notes for her speech.

Sunday morning, Susannah woke feeling sluggish and out of sorts. She realized almost instantly the source of her discomfort. This afternoon, she would confront Nate. For the past two days, she'd gone over in her mind exactly what she planned to say, how she would act.

Nate arrived at four-thirty. She answered his knock, dressed in navy blue slacks and a cream shell-knit sweater. Her hair was neatly rolled into a chignon.

"Susannah." His gaze was hungry as he stepped across the threshold and reached for her.

It was too late to hide her reaction by the time she realized he intended to kiss her. He swept her into his arms and eagerly pressed his mouth over hers. Despite all that he'd failed to tell her, Susannah felt an immediate warm response she couldn't disguise.

Nate threaded his fingers through her hair, removing the pins that held it in place, while he leisurely moved his mouth over hers.

"Two days have never seemed so long," he breathed, then nibbled on her lower lip as if she were a delectable feast and he was a starved man.

Regaining her composure, she broke away, her shoulders heaving. "Would you like some coffee?"

"No. The only thing I want is you."

She started to walk away from him, but Nate reached out and caught her, hauling her back into the warm shelter of his arms. He linked his hands at the small of her back and gazed down at her, his eyes caressing and gentle. Gradually, his expression altered.

"Is everything all right?" he asked.

"Yes...and no," she admitted dryly. "I happened upon an article in an old issue of *Business Monthly*. Does that tell you anything?"

He hesitated, and for a long moment Susannah wondered if he was going to say anything or not.

"So you know?"

"That you're the world's cookie king, or once were—yes, I know."

His eyes narrowed slightly. "Are you angry?"

She sighed. A good deal depended on her delivery, and although she'd practiced her words several times, it was far more difficult than she'd realized. She was determined, however, to remain calm and casual.

"I'm more embarrassed than amused," she said. "I wish you'd said something before I made such a fool of myself."

"Susannah, I know you have every right to be upset." He released her and rubbed the back of his neck as he began to walk back and forth between the living room and kitchen. "It isn't like it was a deep dark secret. I sold the business almost six months ago, and I was taking a sabbatical—hell, I needed one. I'd driven myself as far as I could. My doctor thinks I was on the verge of a complete physical collapse. When I met you, I was just coming out of it, learning how to enjoy life all over again. The last thing I wanted to do was sit down and talk about the past thirteen years. I'd put Rainy Day Cookies behind me, and I was looking to build a new life."

Susannah crossed her arms. "Did you ever intend to tell me?"

"Yes!" he said vehemently. "Thursday night. You were so sweet to have offered me a job and I knew I had to say something then, but you were..."

"Tipsy," she finished for him.

"All right, tipsy, for lack of a better word. You've got to understand why I didn't. The timing was all wrong."

"You must have got a good laugh from the cookie disaster," she said, and was surprised at how steady her voice remained. Her poise didn't even slip, and she was proud of herself.

The edges of his mouth quivered slightly, and it was apparent that he was struggling not to laugh.

"Go ahead," she said, waving her hand dramatically. "I suppose those charred cookies and the smoldering cookie sheets were a comical sight. I don't blame you. I'd probably be in hysterics if the situation was reversed."

"It isn't that. The fact that you made those cookies was one of the sweetest things anyone has ever done for me. I want you to know I was deeply touched."

"I didn't do it for you," she said, struggling to keep the anger out of her voice. "It was a trial by fire—" Realizing what she'd said, Susannah closed her eyes and stopped abruptly.

"Susannah—"

"You must have got a real kick out of that little pep talk I gave you the other day, too. Imagine *me* talking to you about drive, motivation and goals."

"That touched me, too," he insisted.

"Right on the funny bone, I'll bet." She faked a laugh herself just to prove what a good sport she was. She could take a joke, but she wasn't exactly keen on being the brunt of one.

Nate paused, then gestured at her. "I realize it looks bad when you consider it from your point of view."

"Looks bad," she echoed, with a short hysterical laugh. "That's one way of putting it!"

Nate strode from one end of the room to the other. If he didn't stop soon, he was going to wear a hole in the carpet.

"Are you willing to put this small misunderstanding behind us, Susannah, or are you going to hold it against me? Are you willing to ruin what we have over a mistake?"

"I don't know yet." Actually she did, but she didn't want him to accuse her of making snap decisions. It would be so easy for Nate to talk his way out of this. But Susannah had been humiliated. How could she possibly trust him now? He'd thought nothing of hiding a large portion of his life from her.

"How long will it be before you come to a conclusion about us?"

"I don't know that, either."

"I suppose dinner is out?"

She nodded, her face muscles so tight, they ached.

"Okay, think matters through. I trust you to be completely fair and unbiased. All I want you to do is ask yourself something. If the situation were reversed, how would you have handled it?"

"All right." She was willing to grant him that much, although she already knew what she would have done—and it wasn't keep up a charade the way he had.

"There's something else I want you to think about," he said when she held open the door for him.

"What?" Susannah was frantic to get him out of her home quickly. The longer he stayed, the more difficult it was to remain angry with him.

"This." He kissed her then and it was the type of kiss that drove to the very depths of her soul. His mouth on hers was hot, the kiss deep and moist and so filled with longing that her knees almost buckled. Tiny sounds interrupted the moment, and Susannah realized she was the one making them.

When Nate released her, she backed away and nearly stumbled. Breathing hard, she braced her back against the doorframe and heaved in giant gulps of oxygen.

Satisfied, Nate smiled infuriatingly. "Admit it, Susannah," he whispered and ran his index finger over the shell sweater at her collarbone. "We were meant for each other."

"I . . . I'm not willing to admit anything."

His expression looked forlorn. It was no doubt calculated to evoke sympathy, but it wouldn't work. Susannah wouldn't be fooled a second time.

"You'll phone me?" he pressed.

"Yes." When the moon was in the seventh house, which should be somewhere around the time the government balanced the budget. Perhaps in the year two thousand.

FOR TWO DAYS, Susannah's life returned to a more normal routine. She went in to the office early and stayed late, doing everything she could to avoid Nate, although she was certain he would wait patiently for some signal from her. After all, he, too, had his pride—she was counting on that.

When she arrived home on Wednesday, there was a folded note taped to her door. Susannah stared at it for several thundering heartbeats before she reached for it.

She waited until she had put her dinner in the microwave before she read it. Her heart was pounding painfully hard as she folded open the sheet and saw three words: "Call me. Please."

Susannah gave a short hysterical laugh. Ha! Nate Townsend could tumble into a vat of melted chocolate chips before she'd call him again. More than likely he'd say or do something that would remind her of what a fool she'd been! Damn, she thought, but it was hard to stay angry with him.

When the phone rang she was still ambivalent. Jumping back, she glared at it before answering.

"Hello," she said cautiously, quaveringly.

"Susannah? Is that you?"

"Oh, hi, Emily."

"Good grief, you gave me a scare. I thought you were sick. You sounded so feeble."

"No. No, I'm fine."

"I hadn't talked to you in a while and I was wondering how you were doing."

"Fine," she repeated.

"Susannah!" Her sister made her name like a warning. "I know you well enough to realize something is wrong. I also know it probably has something to do with Nate. You haven't mentioned him the last few times we've talked, but before you seemed to be overflowing with things you wanted to say about him."

"I'm not seeing much of Nate these days."

"Why not?"

"Well, being a multimillionaire keeps him busy."

Emily paused long enough to gulp in a breath, then gasped, "I think there must be something wrong with the phone. I thought you just said—"

"Ever been to Rainy Day Cookies?"

"Of course. Hasn't everyone?"

"Have you made the connection yet?"

"You mean Nate..."

"...is Mr. Chocolate Chip himself."

"But that's marvelous. That's wonderful. Why, he's famous... I mean his cookies are world-renowned. To think that the man who developed Rainy Day Cookies actually helped Robert carry out Michelle's crib. I can't wait until he hears this."

"Personally, I wasn't all that impressed." It was difficult to remain indifferent when her sister was bubbling over with such enthusiasm. Emily usually only got excited over something organic.

"When did you find out?" Emily asked, her voice almost accusing, as if Susannah had been holding out on her.

"Last Friday. John Hammer gave me a magazine that had an article about Nate in it. The issue was a few years old, but the article told me everything Nate should have."

A short soft sound of exclamation followed. "So you just found out yourself?"

"Right."

"And you're angry with him?"

"Good heavens, no. Why should I be?" Susannah was afraid Emily wouldn't appreciate the sarcasm.

"He probably planned on telling you," Emily argued, defending Nate. "I don't know your neighbor all that well, but he seemed straightforward enough to me. I'm sure he intended to explain the situation when the time was right."

"Perhaps," Susannah agreed, but as far as she was concerned, that consolation was too little, too late. "Listen, I've got something cooking in the microwave, so I've got to scoot." The excuse was weak, but Susannah didn't want to discuss Nate right now. "Oh, before I forget," she added quickly. "I've got a speaking engagement on the seventeenth, but I'll be finished before five-thirty so you can count on me watching Michelle."

"Great. Listen, sis, if you want to talk, I'm always here. I mean that. What are sisters for if not to talk?"

"Thanks, I'll remember that."

Once she replaced the telephone receiver, Susannah was left to deal, once more, with Nate's short note. By all rights, she should crumple it into a ball and toss it in the garbage. She did, feeling a small, damn small, sense of satisfaction.

Out of sight, out of mind—or so the old adage went—only this time it wasn't working. Every time she turned around the sight of the telephone seemed to pull at her.

Her dinner was cooked, but as she gazed down at the unappetizing entrée, she considered throwing it out and going to the Western Avenue Deli for a pastrami on rye instead. That would serve two purposes; first, it would take her away from the phone, which seemed to want to lure her to its side; and second, she'd at least have a decent meal.

Having made her decision, she was already in the living room when the doorbell chimed. Susannah groaned, knowing even before she answered it that her visitor had to be Nate.

"You didn't call," he snapped the minute she opened the door.

He stormed inside without waiting for an invitation, looking irritated, but in control. "Just how long are you planning to keep me waiting? It's obvious you're intent on making me pay for the error of my ways, which to a certain point I can understand. But we've gone well past that point. So what are you waiting for? An apology? All right—I'm sorry."

"Ah—"

"You have every reason to be upset, but what do you want? Blood? Enough is enough. I'm crazy about you, woman, and you feel the same way about me, so don't try to fool me with this indifference routine, because I can see right through it. Let's put this foolishness behind us and get back on track."

"Why?" she demanded.

"Why what?"

"Why did you wait? Why couldn't you have said something sooner?"

He gave her a look that suggested they were rehashing old news, then started his pacing routine. "Because I wanted to put Rainy Day Cookies out of my mind. I'd made the business my entire world." He stopped and whirled to face her. "I recognized a kindred spirit in you. Your entire life is wrapped up in some sporting goods company—"

"Not just *some* sporting goods company" she returned, indignant. "H&J Lima is the largest in the country."

"Forgive me, Susannah, but that doesn't really impress me. What about your life? Your whole world revolves around how far you can climb up the corporate ladder. Let me tell you that once you're at the top, the view isn't all that great. You forget what it means to appreciate the simple things in life. I did."

"Are you telling me to stop and smell the flowers? Well, I've got news for you, Nate Townsend. I like my life just the way it is. I consider it insulting that you think you can casually walk into my world and my career and insist I'm headed down the road to destruction, because I'll tell you right now—" she paused long enough to gulp in a breath "—I don't appreciate it."

Nate's expression tightened. "I'm not talking about flowers, Susannah. I want you to look out this window at Puget Sound and see something beyond a lovely view with ferryboats and snowcapped mountains. Life is more than that spider gracefully spinning its web in the corner of the balcony. Those are everyday miracles right at our doorstep, but life, abundant life, is more than that. It's meaningful relationships. Friends. Fun. We'd both lost sight of that. It happened to me first, and I can see you headed in the same shattering direction."

"That's all fine and dandy for you, but I—"

"You need the same things I do. We need each other."

"Correction," she said heatedly. "I happen to like my life just the way it is, thank you. And why shouldn't I? My five-year goals have been achieved, and there are more in the making. I can go straight to the top with this company, and that's exactly what I want. As for needing relationships, you're wrong about that, too. I got along just fine before I met you, and the same will prove true when you're out of my life."

The room went so still that for a second Susannah was convinced Nate had stopped breathing.

"When I'm out of your life," he echoed. "I see. So you've made your decision."

"Yes," she said, holding her head high. "It was fun while it lasted, but if I had to choose between you and the vice presidency, the decision wouldn't be the least bit difficult. I'm sure you'll encounter some other young woman who needs saving from herself and her goals. As far as I can see, our relationship was more of a rescue mission, from your perspective,. Now that you know how the cookie crumbles—the pun's intended—then perhaps you'll kindly leave me to my sad sorry lot."

"Susannah, would you listen to me?"

"No." She held up her hand for effect. "I'll try to be happy," she said, a heavy note of mockery in her voice.

For a long moment, Nate said nothing. "You're making a mistake, but that's something you're going to have to learn on your own."

"I suppose you're planning on being around to pick up the pieces when I fall apart?"

His blue eyes narrowed and bored into hers. "I might be, but then again, I might not."

"Well, you needn't worry, because either way, you've got a long wait."

CHAPTER TEN

"Ms Simmons, Mr. Hammer, it's an honor to meet you."

"Thank you," Susannah said, smiling politely at the young man who had been sent to greet her and her employer. The Seattle Convention Center was filled almost to capacity. The moment Susannah realized her audience was going to be so large, her stomach was attacked by a bad case of nerves. Not the most pleasant conditions under which to be eating lunch.

"If you'll come this way, I'll show you to the head table."

Susannah and John Hammer followed the young executive toward the front of the crowded room. There were several others already seated on the stage. Susannah recognized the mayor and a couple of city councillors, along with the King County executive and two prominent local businessmen.

Susannah was assigned the chair to the right of the podium. John was assigned the place beside her. After briefly shaking hands with the conference coordinator, she greeted the others and took her seat. Almost immediately, the caterers started serving lunch, which consisted of an elegantly prepared salad, wild rice and broiled fresh salmon drenched with raspberry vinegar

She didn't think she could manage even a bite while sitting in front of so many people. Glancing out over the sea of unfamiliar faces, she forced herself to remain calm and collected. She was, after all, one of the featured speakers for the afternoon, and she had come well prepared.

There was a slight commotion to the right of her, but the podium blocked her view.

"Hi, gorgeous. No one told me you were going to be here."

Nate. Susannah nearly swallowed her forkful of salmon whole. It stuck in her throat and she would have choked had she not reached for her water glass and hurriedly taken a swallow.

Twisting around in her chair, she came eye to eye with him. "Hello, Nate," she said as nonchalantly as she could. Her smile was firmly rooted in place; explosives couldn't have budged it.

"I thought Nate Townsend might be here," John whispered, looking pleased with himself.

"I see you've taken to following me around now," Nate taunted.

Susannah ignored that comment and both men, studiously returning to her salmon, hoping to suggest that her meal was far more appealing than their conversation.

"Have you missed me?"

It was ten tortuous days since she'd last seen Nate. Avoiding him hadn't been easy. He'd made sure of that. The first night she'd come home to an Italian opera played just loud enough to be heard through her kitchen wall. The sound of the music was combined with the tangy scent of his homemade spaghetti sauce. The aroma of simmering tomatoes and herbs mingled with the pungent scent of hot garlic and butter.

Evidently Nate assumed the way to *her* heart was through her stomach. She'd nearly succumbed then, but her conviction was strong and she'd hurried to a favorite Italian restaurant to alleviate her sudden craving for pasta.

By the weekend, Susannah would have sworn Nate had whipped up every recipe in an entire cookbook, each one more enticing than the last. Susannah had never eaten as many restaurant meals as she had in the past week.

When Nate realized she couldn't be bought so easily with fine food, wine and song—or in this case opera— he tried another tactic, this one less subtle.

A single red rose was waiting for her outside her door when she arrived home from the office. There wasn't any note with it, just a perfect fresh flower. She picked it up and against her better judgment took it inside with her, holding it and inhaling the delicate scent. The only person who could have left it was Nate. In a flurry of righteousness, she'd taken the rose and placed it back where she found it. Five minutes later, she jerked open her door and to her dismay discovered the flower was still there, looking forlorn and dejected.

Deciding to deliver her own less than subtle message, Susannah left the rose outside Nate's door. She hoped he understood once and for all that she refused to be bought!

Nate, however, wasn't easily dissuaded. The rose was followed the next evening by a small box of luscious chocolates. This time Susannah didn't even bring them inside, but marched them directly to Nate's door.

"No," she said now, forcing her thoughts back to the present and the conference. She chanced a look around the crowded, noisy room. "I haven't missed you in the least."

"You haven't?" He looked dashed. "But I thought you were trying to make everything up to me. Why else would you leave those gifts outside my door?"

For just a second her heart thumped wildly. Then she gave him a fiery glare and diligently returned to her meal, making sure she downed every bite. If she didn't, Nate would be sure to think she was lovesick for want of him.

Her employer tilted his head toward her, looking pleased with himself. "I thought it would be a nice surprise for you to be speaking with Nate. Fact is, I arranged it myself."

"How thoughtful," Susannah murmured.

"You have missed me, haven't you?" Nate asked again, balancing on two legs of his chair in an effort to see her.

Okay, she was willing to admit she had been a bit lonely, but that was to be expected. For several weeks, Nate had filled every spare moment of her time with such silliness as baseball games and kite flying. But she'd lived a perfectly fine life before she met him, and now she'd returned to that same serene life-style without a qualm. Her world was wonderful. Complete. She didn't need him to make her a whole person. Nate was going to a great deal of trouble to force her to admit she was miserable without him. She wasn't about to do that.

"I miss you," he said, batting his baby blues at her. "The least you could do is concede you're as lonely and miserable as me."

"But I'm not," she answered sweetly, silently acknowledging the white lie. "I have a fantastic job and a promising career. What else could I want?"

"Children?"

She shook her head. "Michelle and I have lots of fun together, and when we grow bored with each other, she goes home to her mother. As far as I can see that's the perfect way to enjoy a child."

The first speaker approached the podium, and Susannah's attention was diverted to him. He was five minutes into his greetings when Susannah felt something hit her arm. She darted a glance at Nate, who was holding up a white linen napkin. *"What about a husband?"* was inked across the polished cloth.

Groaning, Susannah prayed no one else saw his note, especially her boss. She rolled her eyes and emphatically shook her head. It was then that she noted how everyone was applauding and looking in her direction as though anticipating something. She blinked, not understanding, until she realized that she'd just been introduced and they were waiting for her to stand up and give her talk.

Scraping back her chair, she stood abruptly and approached the podium, not daring to glance at Nate. The man was infuriating! A lesser woman would have dumped the contents of her water glass over his smug head. Instead of venting her irritation, she drew in a deep calming breath and looked out over her audience. She soon realized that was a mistake. There were so many faces, and they all had their eyes trained on her.

Her talk had been carefully planned and memorized. But to be on the safe side, she'd brought the typed sheets with her. She had three key points she intended to share, and had illustrated each one with several colorful anecdotes. Suddenly her mind was a blank. It took every bit of courage she possessed not to bolt and run from the stage.

"Go get 'em, Susannah," Nate whispered, smiling up at her.

His eyes were so full of encouragement and faith that the paralysis started to leave her. Although she'd memorized her speech, she reached for the written version. The instant she read the first sentence she knew she was going to be fine.

For the next twenty minutes she spoke of the importance of indelibly marking a goal on one's mind and how to mentally minimize difficulties and maximize strengths. She closed by explaining the significance of building a mental ladder to one's dreams. She talked about using determination, discipline, dedication and demeanor as the rungs of this cerebral ladder to success.

Despite Nate's earlier efforts to undermine her dignity and poise, she was pleased by the way her speech was received. Many of her listeners nodded at key points in her talk, and Susannah knew she was reaching them. When she finished, she felt good, satisfied with her speech and with herself.

As she turned to go back to her seat, her gaze caught Nate's. He was smiling as he applauded, and the gleam in his eyes was unmistakably one of respect and admiration. The warm, caressing look he offered her nearly tripped her heart into overdrive. Yet he'd maddened her with his senseless questions, distracted her, teased and taunted her with his craziness and then written a note on a napkin. But when she finished her speech, the first person she'd looked to, whether consciously or unconsciously, was Nate.

The man was driving her straight to the loony bin.

Once Susannah was seated, she noted that her hands were trembling. But she couldn't be sure if it was a release from the tension that had gripped her when she first started to speak, or the result of Nate's tender look.

Nate was introduced next, and he approached the podium. It would serve him right, Susannah thought, if she started inking messages on her napkin and holding them up for him to read while he gave his talk. Almost immediately she was shocked by the childishness of the idea. Five minutes with Nate seemed to reduce her mentality to that of a ten-year-old.

With a good deal of ceremony, or so it seemed to Susannah, Nate retrieved his notes from inside his suit jacket. It was all she could do to keep from laughing out loud when she noticed that everything he planned to say had been jotted on the back of a single index card. So this was how seriously he'd taken this afternoon's address. It looked as if he'd scribbled a couple of notes while she was delivering her speech. He hadn't given his lecture a second thought until five minutes before he was supposed to stand before the podium.

Nate proved her wrong, as seemed to be his habit, she thought testily. The minute he opened his mouth, he had the audience in the palm of his hand. Rarely had she heard a more dynamic speaker. His strong voice carried to the farthest corner of the huge hall, and although he used the microphone, Susannah doubted he really needed it.

Nate told of his own beginnings, of how his father had died the year he was to enter college, so that the funds he'd expected to further his education were no longer available. It was the lowest point of his life and out of it had come his biggest success. Then he explained that his mother's chocolate chip cookies had always been everyone's favorite. Because of his father's untimely death, she had taken a job in a local factory, and Nate, eager to find a way to attend the university in the fall, had taken to baking the cookies and selling them to tourists for fifty cents each.

Halfway through the summer he'd made more than enough money to see him through his first year of schooling. Soon a handful of local delis had contacted him, wanting to include his cookies as part of their menus. These requests were followed by others from restaurants and hotels. He had been approached by a small cookie company that wanted his recipe for chocolate chip, as well as peanut butter cookies.

Nate went to school that first year and took every business course available to him. By the end of the following summer, he had set up a kitchen and opened his own business, which thrived despite his mistakes. The rest was history. By the time he graduated from college, Nate was already a millionaire. To his credit, he'd resisted the temptation to abandon his education. It had served him well since, and he was pleased he'd stuck with it, even though everyone around him seemed to be saying that he knew more, from personal experience, than most of the authors of the textbooks did. A fact he was quick to dispute.

Susannah was enthralled. She'd assumed Nate would be telling this audience what he'd been beating her over the head with from the moment they'd met—that the drive to succeed was all fine and good, but worthless if in the process one forgot who and what one was. However, if that thought was on Nate's mind, he didn't voice it. Susannah suspected he'd reserved that philosophy for her and her alone.

When he returned to his seat, the applause was thunderous. The first thing he did was look to Susannah, who smiled softly, as touched as the rest of his audi-

ence by his personal experiences. Not once had he patted himself on the back, or taken credit for the
phenomenal success of Rainy Day Cookies. Susannah
would almost have preferred it if his talk had been a
boring rambling account of his prosperous career. She
didn't want to feel so much admiration for him. It
would be easier to work Nate out of her life and her
mind if she didn't.

The luncheon ended a few minutes later. Gathering
up her things, Susannah hoped to make a speedy escape. She should have known that Nate wouldn't allow
that. Several people had hurried up to the podium to
talk to him, but he excused himself and moved to her
side.

"Susannah, I'd like to talk to you."

She made a show of glancing at her watch, then at her
boss. "I have another appointment," she said stiffly.
She secured the strap of her purse over her shoulder and
offered him what she hoped resembled a regretful smile.
"Your speech was wonderful."

"Thank you, so was yours," she said, then mentioned the one thing that had troubled her. "You never
told me about your father's death."

"I've never told you that I love you, but I do."

His words, so casual, so calm and serene, were like a
blow to her solar plexus. Susannah felt the tears form
in her eyes and tried to blink them back. "I...I wish you
hadn't said that."

"The way I feel about you isn't going to change."

"I...really have to go," she said, glancing anx-
iously toward John Hammer. All she wanted to do was
escape with her heart intact.

"Mr. Townsend," a woman bellowed from the audience. "You're going to be at the auction tonight, aren't you?"

Nate's gaze slid reluctantly from Susannah to the well-dressed woman on the floor. "I'll be there," he called back.

"I'll be looking for you," she said and laughed girlishly.

Susannah couldn't help thinking that the other woman's laugh resembled the sound an unwell rooster would make. She was tempted to ask Nate exactly what kind of auction he planned to attend where he expected to run into someone who yelled questions across a crowded room. But she resisted the urge, which was just as well.

"Goodbye, Nate," she said, turning away.

"Goodbye, my love." It wasn't until she was walking out of the Convention Center that Susannah realized how final his farewell had sounded.

It was what she wanted, wasn't it? As far as she was concerned, Nate had proved he wasn't trustworthy; he had an infuriating habit of keeping secrets. So now that he wasn't planning on seeing her again, there was absolutely no reason for her to complain. At least that was what Susannah told herself as she headed home, taking a short side trip down by the Seattle waterfront.

Within a couple of hours, Emily and Robert would be dropping off Michelle before they went to dinner with Robert's employer. Once the baby was with her, Susannah reminded herself, there wouldn't be time to worry about Nate or anyone else.

By the time Emily arrived with her family, Susannah was in a rare mood. She felt light-headed and witty, as though she'd downed something alcoholic, but the strongest thing she'd had all evening was coffee.

"Hi," she greeted cheerfully, opening the door. Michelle looked at her with large round eyes and grabbed for her mother's coat collar.

"Sweetheart, this is your Auntie Susannah, remember?"

"Emily, the only thing she remembers is that every time you bring her here, you leave," Robert said, carrying in the diaper bag and a sack full of blankets and toys.

"Hello, Robert," Susannah murmured, kissing him on the cheek. The action surprised her as much as it did her brother-in-law. "I understand congratulations are in order."

"For you, too."

"Yes, well, it was nothing."

"Not according to the article in the paper."

"Oh," Emily said, whirling around. "Speaking of the newspaper, I read Nate's name this evening."

"Yes . . . we were both speakers at a conference this afternoon."

Emily looked impressed, but Susannah couldn't be sure if it was for her or for Nate.

"That wasn't what I read about him," Emily continued, focusing her attention on removing the jacket from Michelle's stubby arms. The child wasn't the least bit cooperative. "Nate's involved in the auction."

"Da-da!" Michelle cried once her arms were free.

Robert looked on proudly. "She finally learned my name. Michelle's first and only word," he added, beaming. "Da-da loves his baby, yes he does."

It was so unusual to hear Robert speaking baby talk that for an instant, Susannah didn't catch what her sister was saying. "What was that?"

"I'm trying to tell you about the auction," Emily said again, as if that should explain everything. At Susannah's puzzled look, she added, "His name was in an article about the auction to benefit the Children's Home Society."

The light bulb that clicked on inside Susannah's head was powerful enough to search the night sky. "Not the *bachelor* auction?" Her question was little more than a husky murmur. No wonder the woman who'd shouted to Nate at the luncheon had been so brazen! She was going to bid on him.

Slowly, hardly conscious of what she was doing, Susannah lowered herself onto the sofa next to her sister.

"He didn't tell you?"

"No, but then why should he? We're nothing more than neighbors."

"Susannah!"

Her sister had the infuriating habit of making an entire statement just by the way she said Susannah's name.

"Honey," Robert said, studying his watch, "we'd better leave now if we intend to be at the restaurant on time. I don't want to keep my boss waiting."

Emily's glance toward Susannah promised a long talk later. At least Susannah had several hours during which to come up with a way of warding off her sister's questions.

"Have a good time, you two," Susannah said lightheartedly, guiding them toward the door, "and don't you worry about a thing."

"Bye, Michelle," Emily said and waved from the doorway.

"Tell Mommy goodbye." Since the baby didn't seem too cooperative, Susannah held up the chubby hand and waved it for her.

As soon as Emily and Robert had left, Michelle started whimpering softly. Susannah took one look at her niece and her spirits plummeted. Whom was she trying to fool? Herself? She'd been miserable and lonely from the moment she left Nate. Michelle sniffled, and Susannah felt like crying right along with her.

So the notorious Nate Townsend had done it again—he hadn't even bothered to mention the bachelor auction. Obviously he'd agreed to this event weeks in advance and it had never even occurred to him to tell her. Oh, sure, he swore undying love to her, but he was willing to let some strange woman buy him. Men, she was quickly learning, were not to be trusted.

The more Susannah thought back over the details of this evening, the more infuriated she became. When she'd asked Nate about helping her out with Michelle, he'd casually mentioned that he had "something else on" this evening. He sure did. Auctioning off his body to the highest bidder, and all in the name of charity!

"I told him I didn't want to see him again," Susannah announced to her niece, her fervor causing her to raise her voice. "That man was trouble from the moment we met. You were with me at the time, remember? Don't we wish we'd known then what we know now?"

Michelle's shoulders bobbed up and down with the effort to either cry or keep from crying. Susannah didn't know which.

"He had this habit of hiding things from me. Important information, but I'm telling you right now that I've completely washed that man out of my hair. Any woman who wants him tonight can have him, because I'm not interested.''

Michelle buried her face against Susannah's neck.

''I know exactly how you feel, kid,'' she said, continuing to stalk the carpet in front of the large picture window. The night was filled with the sights and sounds of the city. ''It's like you've lost your best friend, right?''

''Da-da.''

''He's with your mommy. I thought Nate was my friend once,'' she said to the baby sadly. ''But I learned the hard way what he really was—nothing earth-shattering, don't misunderstand me. But he let me make a complete idiot of myself.''

Michelle stared up at Susannah, apparently enthralled with her speech. In an effort to keep the baby appeased, she continued chattering. ''I hope he feels like a fool on the auction block tonight,'' she said, imagining him standing in front of an auditorium full of screaming women. She slowly released a sigh when she realized that with his good looks, Nate would probably bring in top money. In past year's auctions, several of the men had gone for as much as a thousand dollars. All for an evening in the company of one of Seattle's eligible bachelors.

''So much for undying love and devotion,'' she muttered. Michelle continued to stare at her, and Susannah felt it was her duty as the baby's aunt to give this little one some free advice. ''Men aren't all they're cracked up to be. You'd be wise to learn that now.''

Michelle gurgled cheerfully, obviously in full agreement.

''I for one don't need a man. I'm completely and utterly happy living on my own. I've got a job, a really good job, and a few close friends—mostly people I work with—and of course your mother." Michelle raised her hand to Susannah's face and rubbed her cheek where a tear had streaked a moist trail.

"I know what you're thinking," Susannah added before she realized that it was unnecessary to explain anything to anyone so young. "If I'm so happy, then why am I crying? Darned if I know. The problem is I can't help loving him and that's what makes this all so difficult. Then he had to go and write me that note on a napkin." She paused and pressed her fingers to her mouth to calm herself. "He asked me if I was willing to live my life without a husband . . . on a napkin he asked me that. Can you imagine what the caterers are going to think when they read that? And we were sitting at the head table, no less."

"Da-da."

"He asked about that, too," Susannah explained, sniffling as she spoke. She was silent a moment and when she began again her voice trembled slightly. "I never thought I'd want children, but then I didn't realize how much I could love a little one like you." Holding the baby against her breast, Susannah closed her eyes to the tight pain that clawed at her. "I could just shoot that man."

Enthralled with Susannah's hair, Michelle reached up and tugged it free from the confining pins.

"I wore it up this afternoon just to be contrary and prove to myself that I'm my own woman, and then he was there and the whole time I was speaking I wished I'd left it down—just because Nate prefers it that way. Oh, honestly, Michelle, I think I may be ready to go off the deep end here. Any advice you'd care to lend me?"

"Da-da."

"That's what I thought you'd say." Forcing in a deep breath, Susannah tried to control the tears that sprang to her eyes. She hadn't expected to cry. The tears had taken her by surprise, and she had yet to understand their significance.

"I thought once I was promoted to vice president everything would be so wonderful and, well, it has been good, but I feel so empty inside. Oh, Michelle, I don't know if I can explain it. The nights are so long and there are only so many hours I can work anymore without thinking of getting home and the possibility of seeing Nate. I...I seem to have lost my drive. Here I was talking to all these people today about determination and drive and discipline and none of it seemed real. Then...then on the way home I was walking along the waterfront and I saw an old college friend. She's married and has a baby a little older than you and she looked so happy." She paused long enough to rub the back of her hand under her nose. "I told her all about my big promotion and Sally seemed genuinely happy for me, but I felt this giant hole inside me."

"Da-da."

"Michelle, can't you learn another word? Please. How about Auntie? It's not so difficult. Say it after me. Auntie."

"Da-da."

"Nate is probably going to meet some gorgeous blonde and fall madly in love with her. She'll bid hundreds of dollars for him and he'll be so impressed that he won't even mind when she keeps him captive until—" Susannah stopped abruptly, her mind whirling. Her head snapped up and her back straightened. "You won't believe what I was just thinking," she said to Michelle, who was studying her curiously. "It's completely crazy, but then again, perhaps not."

Michelle waved her arms and actually seemed interested in hearing about this insane idea that had popped into Susannah's head. It was impossible. Absurd. But then she'd made a fool of herself over Nate so many times that once more certainly wasn't going to hurt.

It took several minutes to get Michelle back into her coat. Susannah would have sworn the contraption had more arms and legs than a centipede.

After glancing at the balance in her checkbook, she grabbed her savings-account records and, carrying Michelle, headed to the parking garage. She'd been saving up to pay cash for a new car, but bidding for Nate was more important.

The parking lot outside the theater where the bachelor auction was being held was filled to capacity, and Susannah had a terrible time finding a place to leave her car. Once she was inside the main entrance, the doorman was hesitant to let her into the auditorium, since Michelle was with her and neither one of them had a ticket.

"Lady, I'm sorry, I can't let you in there without a ticket and a bidding number—besides I don't think married women are allowed."

"I'll buy one and this is my niece. Now either you let me in there or... or you'll... I'll... I don't know what I'll do. Come on," she pleaded. "This is a matter of life and death." Okay, so that was a slight exaggeration.

While the doorman conferred with his supervisor, Susannah looked through the swinging doors that led into the theater. She watched as several women raised their hands, and leaped enthusiastically to their feet to show their numbers. A television crew was there taping the proceedings, as well.

Susannah was impatiently bouncing Michelle on her hip when the doorman returned.

"Ma'am, I'm sorry, but my supervisor says the tickets are sold out."

Susannah was about to argue with him when she heard the master of ceremonies call out Nate's name. A fervent murmur rose from the crowd.

Desperate times demanded desperate measures, and instead of demurely going back outside, Susannah rushed to the swinging doors, tossed them open and hurried down the narrow aisle.

As soon as the doorman saw what she'd done, he ran after her and shouted, "Stop that woman!"

Abruptly, the master of ceremonies ceased speaking, and a hush fell over the room as every head in the place turned toward Susannah, who was clutching Michelle protectively to her chest. She'd made it halfway down the center aisle before the doorman caught up with her. Susannah cast a wretched pleading glance at Nate, who had shielded his eyes from the glare of the lights and was staring at her.

Michelle cooed, having enjoyed the game of cat and mouse. With her pudgy hand, she pointed toward Nate.

"Da-da! Da-da!" she cried, and her voice seemed as loud as a sonic boom.

CHAPTER ELEVEN

AN IMMEDIATE UPROAR rose from the theater full of women. Nothing Susannah did could distract Michelle from pointing toward Nate and calling him Da-Da. For his part, Nate appeared to be taking all the commotion in his stride. He walked over to the master of ceremonies, whom Susannah recognized as Cliff Dolittle, a local television personality, and whispered something in his ear.

"What seems to be the problem here?" Cliff asked.

"This lady doesn't have a ticket or a bidding number," the doorman shouted back. He held Susannah by her upper arm and didn't look any too pleased with this unexpected turn of events.

"I may not have a number, but I've got $6010.12 I'd like to bid for this man," she shouted.

Her announcement was again followed by a hubbub of whispering voices, which rolled over the theater like a wave crashing on the shore. The six thousand was the balance in Susannah's savings account, plus all the cash she was carrying with her.

A noise from the back of the room distracted her, and it was then that she realized the television crew had the cameras rolling. Every single detail of this debacle was being documented.

"I have a bid of $6010.12," Cliff Dolittle announced, sounding a little shocked himself. "Going once, going twice—'' he paused and his gaze scanned the female audience ''—sold to the lady who gate-crashed this auction. The one with the baby in her arms.''

The doorman released Susannah and reluctantly directed her to where she was supposed to pay. It seemed everyone was watching her and whispering. Several of the women were bold enough to shout bits of advice to her.

A man with a camera balanced on his shoulder hurried toward her. Loving the attention, Michelle pointed her finger toward the lens and cried ''Da-da'' once more for all the people who would soon be viewing this disaster at home.

''Susannah, what are you doing here?'' Nate whispered, joining her when she reached the teller's booth.

''You know what really irritates me about this?'' she said, her face bright with embarrassment. ''I could probably have had you for three thousand, only I panicked and offered every penny I have. Me, the financial marketing wizard. I'll never be able to hold my head up again.''

''You're not making the least bit of sense.''

''And you are? One moment you confess undying love to me and the next you're on the auction block, parading around for a bunch of . . . women.''

''That comes to $6025.12,'' the white-haired woman in the teller's booth told her.

''I only bid $6010.12,'' Susannah protested.

''The extra money is the price of the ticket. You weren't supposed to bid without one.''

''I see.''

Unzipping her purse and withdrawing her checkbook while balancing Michelle on her hip proved to be difficult.

"Here, I'll take her." Nate reached for Michelle, who surprised them both by protesting loudly.

"What have you been telling her about me?" Nate teased.

"The truth." With a good deal of ceremony, Susannah wrote out the check and ripped it from her book. Reluctantly she slid it across the short counter toward the woman collecting the fees.

"I'll write you a receipt."

"Thank you," Susannah said absently. "By the way, what exactly am I getting for my hard-earned money?"

"One evening with this young man."

"One evening," Susannah repeated grimly. "If we go out to dinner does he pay or do I?"

"I do," Nate answered for her.

"It's a good thing, because I don't have any money left."

"Have you eaten?"

"No, and I'm starved."

"Me, too," he told her smiling sheepishly, but the look in his eyes said he wasn't talking about snacking on crepes suzette. "I can't believe you did this."

"I can't, either," she said, shaking her head in wonder. "I'm still reeling with the shock." Later, she'd probably start trembling and not be able to stop. Never in her life had she done anything so bold. Love apparently did this to a woman. Before she met Nate she'd been a sound, logical, dedicated businesswoman. Six weeks later, she was smelling orange blossoms and thinking about weddings and babies and giving up a promising career all because she was in head over heels in love!

"Come on, let's get out of here," Nate said, tucking his hand around her waist and leading her toward the theater doors.

Susannah nodded. The doorman looked pleased that she was leaving his domain.

"Susannah," Nate said, once they were in the parking lot. He turned and placed his hands on her shoulders, then closed his eyes as if gathering together his thoughts. "You were the last person I expected to see tonight."

"Obviously," she returned stiffly. "When we're married, I'm going to have to insist that you keep me informed of your schedule."

Nate's head snapped up. "When we're married?"

"You didn't honestly believe I just spent six thousand dollars for a single dinner in some fancy restaurant, did you?"

"But—"

"And there'll be children, as well. Two are probably about all I can handle, but we'll play that by ear when the time comes."

For the first time since she'd met him, Nate Townsend seemed speechless. His mouth made several movements in an attempt to talk, but no sound came out.

"I suppose you're wondering how I plan to manage my career," she said, before he could ask the question. "I'm not exactly sure what I'm going to do yet. Since I'm looking at the good side of thirty, I suppose we could delay having children for a few more years."

"I'm thirty-three. I want a family soon."

Nate's voice didn't sound at all like it normally did, and Susannah peered at him carefully, wondering if the shock had been too much for him. It had been for her! And she was probably going to end up on the eleven-o'clock news. "All right, we'll plan on starting our family right away," she agreed. "But before we do any more talking about babies, I need to ask you something important. Are you willing to change messy diapers?"

A smile played at the edges of his mouth before he nodded.

"Good." Susannah looked at Michelle, who had laid her head against her aunt's shoulder and closed her eyes. Apparently the events of the evening had tired her out.

"What about dinner?" Nate asked as he tenderly brushed the silky smooth hair from the baby's brow. "Michelle doesn't look like she's going to last much longer."

"Don't worry about it. I'll pick up something on the way home." She paused, then gestured weakly with her hand. "Forget that. I . . . I don't have any money left."

Nate grinned widely. "I'll pick up something and meet you back at your place in half an hour."

Susannah smiled her appreciation. "Thanks."

"No," Nate whispered, his eyes locked with hers. "Thank you."

He kissed her then, slipping his hand behind her neck and tilting her face up to meet his. His touch was so potent Susannah thought her heart would beat itself right out of her chest.

"Nate." Her eyes remained closed when his name parted her lips.

"Hmm?"

"I really do love you."

"Yes, I know. I love you, too. I knew it the night you
bought the stroganoff from the Western Avenue Deli
and tried to make me think you'd whipped it up yourself."

She opened her eyes and raised them, wide and dark,
to him. "But I didn't even realize it then. Why, we
barely knew each other."

He kissed the tip of her nose. "I was aware almost
from the first time we met that my life was never going
to be the same if you weren't there to share it with me."

His romantic words stirred her heart and she wiped a
tear from the corner of her eye. "I...I'd better take
Michelle home," she said, and sniffled.

Nate's thumb wiped the moisture from her cheek before he kissed her again. "I won't be long," he promised.

He wasn't. Susannah had no sooner got Michelle
home and into her sleepers when there was a light knock
at the door.

Hurriedly, she tiptoed across the carpet and opened
it. She pressed her finger to her lips as she let Nate inside.

"I got Chinese."

Her eyes widened as she nodded. "Great."

She paused on her way into the kitchen and showed
him Michelle, who was sleeping soundly on the end of
the sofa. Susannah had taken the opposite cushion and
braced it against the side so there wasn't any chance she
could fall off.

"You're going to be a good mother," he whispered,
kissing her forehead.

It was silly to get all misty-eyed over Nate's saying
something like that, but she did. She succeeded in dis-

guising her emotion by walking into the kitchen and getting two plates from the cupboard. Opening the silverware drawer, she brought out forks, as well.

Nate set the large white sack on the tabletop and lifted out five wire-handled boxes. "Garlic chicken, panfried noodles, ginger beef and two large egg rolls. Do you think that'll be enough?"

"Were you planning on feeding the Seventh Infantry?" she teased.

"You said you were hungry." He opened all the boxes but one.

Susannah filled her plate and sat next to Nate, propping her feet on the cushion of the chair opposite her. The food was delicious, and after the first few mouthfuls she decided if Nate could eat with chopsticks she should try it, too. Her efforts had a humbling effect on her.

Watching her artless movements, Nate laughed, then leaned over and kissed the corner of her mouth.

"What's in there?" she asked pointing a chopstick at the fifth wire-handled box.

He shrugged. "I forget."

Curious, Susannah reached for the container and opened it. Her breath lodged in her throat as she raised her eyes to Nate's. "It's a black velvet box."

"Oh, yes, now that you mention it I remember the chef saying something about black velvet being the special of the month." He paused long enough to answer her question and then went on expertly delivering food to his mouth with the chopsticks.

Susannah continued to stare inside the white carton at the velvet box as if it would leap out and open itself. It was the size of a ring box.

Nate waved a chopstick in her direction. "You might as well take it out and see what's inside."

Wordlessly she did as he suggested. Once the box was free, she set the carton aside and lifted the lid. She gasped when she saw the size of the diamond. For one wild moment she couldn't breathe.

"I picked it up when I was in San Francisco," Nate told her, with as much emotion as if he were discussing the weather.

The solitary diamond held her gaze as effectively as a magnet. "It's the most beautiful ring I've ever seen."

"Me too. I took one look at it and told the jeweler to wrap it up."

He acted so casual about it, seeming far more interested in eating his ginger beef and panfried noodles than discussing anything as mundane as an engagement ring.

"I suppose I might as well mention that while I was in San Francisco, I made an offer for the Cougars. They're a professional baseball team, in case you don't know."

"The baseball team? You're going to own a professional baseball team?" Any news he was going to hit her with, it seemed, was going to be big.

He nodded. "I haven't heard back yet, but if that doesn't work out then I might be able to interest the owner of the New York Wolves in selling."

He made it all sound as if he were discussing buying a car instead of something that cost millions of dollars.

"But whatever happens, we'll make Seattle our home."

Susannah nodded, although she wasn't exactly sure why.

"Here." He set his plate aside and took the ring box from her limp hand. "I suppose the thing to do would be to place this on your finger."

Once again, Susannah nodded. Her meal was sitting like a ton of lead in the pit of her stomach. From habit, she held out her right hand. He grinned and reached for her left one.

"I had to guess the size," he said, deftly removing the diamond from its lush bed. "I had the jeweler make it a size five, because your fingers are dainty." The ring slipped on easily, the fit perfect.

Susannah couldn't stop staring at it. Never in all her life had she dreamed she would ever have anything so beautiful. "I...don't dare go near the water with this," she whispered, looking down at her hand. Lowering her gaze helped cover her sudden welling up of tears. The catch in her voice was telltale enough.

"Not go near the water...why?"

"If I accidentally fell in," she said, forcing a light laugh, "I'd sink from the weight of the diamond."

"Is it too big?"

Quickly she shook her head. "It's perfect."

Catching her unawares, Nate pressed his mouth to her trembling lips, kissing what breath she had completely away. "I planned to ask you to marry me the night I came back from the trip. We were going out for dinner, remember?"

Susannah nodded. That had been shortly after she'd read the article in *Business Monthly* about Nate. The day her whole world had felt as if it were rocking beneath her feet.

"I know we talked briefly about your career, but I have something else I need to tell you."

Susannah nodded, because commenting at this point was becoming increasingly impossible.

"What would it take to lure you away from H&J Lima?"

The diamond on her ring finger seemed more than enough incentive, but she wasn't going to let him know that quite yet. "Why?"

"Because I'm starting a kite company. Actually, it's going to be a nationwide franchise. I've got plans for opening ten stores in strategic cities around the country to see how it flies." He stopped long enough to laugh at his pun. "But from the testing we've been doing, this is going to hit it off big. However—" he paused to draw in a deep breath "—I'm lacking one important part of my team. I need a marketing expert, and was wondering if you'd like to apply for the job."

"I suppose," she said, deciding to play his game. "But I'd want top salary, generous bonuses, a four-day week, a health and retirement plan and adequate maternity leave."

"The job's yours."

"I don't know, Nate, there could be problems," she said, cocking her head to one side, letting him think she was already having second thoughts. "People are going to talk."

"Why?"

"Because I fully intend to sleep with the boss. And some old fuddy-duddy is bound to think that's how I got the job."

"Let them." He laughed, reaching for her, wrapping his arms around her trim waist and hauling her into his lap. "Have I told you I'm crazy about you, woman?"

Smiling into his eyes, she nodded. "One thing I want cleared up before we go any further, Nate Townsend. No more secrets. Understand?"

"Scout's honor." He spit on the end of his fingertips and used the same fingers to cross his heart. "I used to do that when I was a kid. It meant I was serious."

"Well," Susannah murmured, thinking past, "since you seem to be in a pledging mood, there are a few items I'd like to have you swear to."

"Such as?"

"Such as . . ." she whispered, and lowered her mouth to a scant inch above his. Whatever thoughts had been in her mind scattered like autumn leaves caught in a brisk whirlwind. Her tongue outlined his lips, teasing and taunting him as he'd taught her to do.

"Susannah, dear Lord . . ."

Whatever he meant to say was interrupted by the doorbell. Susannah lifted her head. It took a moment to clear her muddled thoughts before she realized it must be her sister and brother-in-law returning from their celebration dinner with Robert's boss.

She tried to move from Nate's lap, but he groaned in protest and tightened his arms around her. "Whoever it is will go away,' he whispered close to her ear.

"Nate—"

"Go back to doing what you were just doing and forget whoever's at the door."

"It's Emily and Robert."

Nate moaned and released her.

Susannah had no sooner unlocked the door than Emily flew into the room as though she were being pursued by a banshee. She marched into the center of the living room, stopped abruptly and looked around.

Robert followed her, looking nearly as frenzied as his wife. Sane sensible Robert!

"What's wrong?" Susannah asked, her heart leaping with concern.

"You're asking *us* that?" Robert flared.

"Now, Robert," Emily said, gently placing her hand on her husband's forearm. "There's no need to be so angry. Stay calm."

"Me? Angry?" he cried facing his wife. "In the middle of our after-dinner drink you let out a shriek that scared me out of ten years of my life and now you're telling me not to be angry?"

"Emily," Susannah tried again, "What's wrong?"

"Is Nate here?" Robert interrupted. One corner of her brother-in-law's mouth curved down in a snarl. He raised his clenched fist. "I'd like ten minutes alone with that man. Give me ten minutes."

"Robert!" Emily and Susannah cried simultaneously.

"Did someone say my name?" Nate asked, as he strolled out from the kitchen.

Emily threw herself in front of her husband, patting his heaving chest with her hands. "Now, honey, settle down. There's no need to get so upset."

Susannah was completely confused. She had never heard her brother-in-law raise his voice before. Whatever had happened had clearly unsettled him to the point of violence.

"He's not going to get away with this," Robert shouted, straining against his wife's restricting hands.

"Away with what?" Nate said with a calm that seemed to inflame Robert even more.

"Taking my daughter away from me."

"What?" Susannah cried. It amazed her that Michelle could be sleeping through all this commotion. But fortunately the baby seemed completely oblivious to what was happening.

"I think you'd better start from the beginning," Susannah instructed, leading everyone into the kitchen. "There's obviously been some kind of misunderstanding. Now sit down and I'll put on some decaffeinated coffee and we can sort this out in a reasonable manner."

Her brother-in-law pulled out a chair and put his elbows on the table, supporting his head in his hands.

"Why don't you start?" Susannah said, looking at her sister.

"Well," Emily began, taking in a deep breath, "as I told you, we were having dinner with Robert's boss and—"

"They know all that," Robert interrupted. "Tell them about the part when we were having a drink in the cocktail lounge."

"Yes," Emily said, heaving a great sigh. "That does seem to be where the problem started, doesn't it?"

Susannah shared a look with Nate, wondering if he was as lost as she was in this muddle. Neither Emily nor Robert was making any sense.

"Go on," Susannah encouraged, growing impatient.

"As I explained, we were all sitting in the cocktail lounge having a drink. There was a television set playing in the corner of the room. I hadn't been paying much attention to it, but I looked up and I saw you and Michelle on the screen."

"That was when she gave a scream that was loud enough to curdle a Bloody Mary," Robert explained. "I

got everyone to be quiet while the announcer came on.
He said that you had taken *my daughter* to this...this
bachelor auction. Then they showed Michelle pointing
her finger at Nate and calling him Da-da.''

"That was when Robert let out a fierce yell," Emily
explained.

"Oh, Lord." Susannah slumped into a chair, wanting to find a hole to crawl into and hibernate for the
next ten years. Maybe by then Seattle would have forgotten how she'd disgraced herself.

"Did they say anything else?" Nate wanted to know,
doing a poor job of disguising his amusement.

"Only that the details would follow at eleven."

"I demand an explanation!" Robert said, looking to
Nate.

"It's all very simple," Susannah rushed to explain.
"See...Nate's wearing a suit that's very similar to
yours. Same shade of brown. From the distance, Michelle obviously mistook him for you."

"She did?" Robert muttered.

"Of course," Susannah went on. "Besides, Da-da is
the only word she can say..." Her voice trailed off.

"Michelle knows who her daddy is," Nate said matter-of-factly. "You don't need to worry that—"

"Susannah," Emily broke in, "when did you get that
diamond? It looks like an engagement ring."

"It is," Nate said and reached to the middle of the
table for the last egg roll. He paused and looked at Susannah. "You don't mind, do you?"

"No. Go ahead."

"What channel was it?" Nate asked between bites.
Emily told him.

"It must be a slow news day," Susannah mumbled.

"Gee, Susannah," said Emily, "I always thought if you were going to make television news it would be over some big business deal. I never dreamed it would be because of a man. Are you going to tell me what happened?"

"Someday," she said, expelling her breath. She'd never dreamed it would be over a man, either, but this one was special. More than special.

"Well, since we're going to be brothers-in-law I guess I can forget about this unfortunate incident," Robert said generously, having regained his composure.

"Good, I'd like to be friends," Nate said, holding out his hand for Robert to shake.

"You're going to be married?" Emily asked her sister.

Susannah exchanged a happy smile with Nate and nodded.

"When?"

"Soon," Nate answered for her. His eyes told her the sooner the better.

She felt the heat crawl into her face, but she was as eager as Nate to get to the altar.

"Not only has Susannah agreed to be my wife, she's also decided to take on the position of marketing director for Windy Day Kites."

"You're leaving H&J Lima?" Robert asked, as if he couldn't believe his ears.

"Had to," she explained. She moved to Nate's side, wrapped her arms around his waist and smiled up at him. "The owner made me an offer I couldn't refuse."

Nate's smile felt like a warm summer day. Susannah closed her eyes, basking in the glow of this man who'd taught her about love and laughter and rainy day kisses

MILLS & BOON®

Next Month's Romances

Each month you can choose from a wide variety of romance novels from Mills & Boon. Below are the new titles to look out for next month from the Presents™ and Enchanted™ series.

Presents™

A NANNY FOR CHRISTMAS	Sara Craven
A FORBIDDEN DESIRE	Robyn Donald
THE WINTER BRIDE	Lynne Graham
THE PERFECT MATCH?	Penny Jordan
RED-HOT AND RECKLESS	Miranda Lee
BARGAIN WITH THE WIND	Kathleen O'Brien
THE DISOBEDIENT BRIDE	Elizabeth Power
ALL MALE	Kay Thorpe

Enchanted™

SANTA'S SPECIAL DELIVERY	Val Daniels
THE MARRIAGE PACT	Elizabeth Duke
A MIRACLE FOR CHRISTMAS	Grace Green
ACCIDENTAL WIFE	Day Leclaire
ONE NIGHT BEFORE CHRISTMAS	Catherine Leigh
A SINGULAR HONEYMOON	Leigh Michaels
A HUSBAND FOR CHRISTMAS	Emma Richmond
TEMPORARY GIRLFRIEND	Jessica Steele

LaVyrle
SPENCER

✳

The Hellion

Two Hearts…Worlds Apart

As teenagers they had shared a wild and reckless love—and had been forced to pay the highest price. Now, three broken marriages later, Tommy Lee Gentry has come knocking on Rachel Hollis' door, begging to be given another another chance.

"LaVyrle Spencer has written a truly special story…The Hellion is nostalgic and captures the feelings of love lost and years wasted…SUPERB!"

—Chicago Sun Times

Jennifer
BLAKE

GARDEN
of
SCANDAL

She wants her life back...

Branded a murderer, Laurel Bancroft has
been a recluse for years. Now she wants her
life back--but someone in her past will do
anything to ensure the truth stays buried.

*"Blake's style is as steamy as a still July
night...as overwhelmingly hot as Cajun spice."*
—Chicago Tribune

**AVAILABLE IN PAPERBACK
FROM NOVEMBER 1997**

GET TO KNOW

THE BEST OF ENEMIES

the latest blockbuster from TAYLOR SMITH

Who would you trust with your life? Think again.

Linked to a terrorist bombing, a young student goes missing. One woman believes in the girl's innocence and is determined to find her before she is silenced. Leya Nash has to decide—quickly—who to trust. The wrong choice could be fatal.

—

Valid only in the UK & Ireland against purchases made in retail outlets and not in conjunction with any Reader Service or other offer.